CLASSIC ADVENTURES

This book belongs to

Name Kyle Reynolds

Date 12/97

King Arthur and his Knights

King Arthur and his Knights

Tales from the Legend

The Classic Adventures Series

First published by Blackie
This facsimile edition
© Fabbri Publishing Ltd 1992
Printed and bound in Spain by Printer
Industria Gráfica, Barcelona

ISBN 1-85587-347-8

KING ARTHUR AND HIS KNIGHTS

CHAPTER I

THE SWORD IN THE STONE

UTHER, King of Britain, had been ill now for many weary months. In the meantime his enemies had grown very strong, and had defeated his army in a great battle. So one of his wise men, Merlin, advised that the King should be carried on a horse litter to the field of battle, that his presence might bring victory to his men.

It had brought victory—victory for which the brave King had to pay dearly. He now lay very ill, and the news ran over the castle that he was worse—that indeed he was like to die.

For the last three days and nights King Uther had been speechless, and as yet he had not named the person who was to succeed to the throne on his death, so the barons went to Merlin to ask his advice. He told them to assemble in the King's chamber at the same hour the next day, and by the grace of God and the aid of his charms he would make the King name the successor to his kingdom.

Next day, at the appointed hour, all the barons, with Merlin, came to the King's chamber. When the door was closed behind them, Merlin drew down his cloak from his face and looked round on the gathered barons and the weeping Queen.

"The King still lives?" he asked in a harsh voice.

"He still lives, but that is all," answered one of the barons. "He has not spoken a word for three days."

Merlin drew near to the King's bed, and a cloud gathered in his eyes as one may gather in the heavens before rain.

"It is the will of all," he said, turning to the Queen and the barons, "that I make the King speak. Shall he name the one who is to succeed him?"

"It is our will," said the barons; and the Queen answered also: "It is our will."

Merlin covered his eyes for a moment, and then, turning toward the bed, "Sire," said he to the King, "is it your will that your son Arthur be king after you?"

These words were scarcely uttered, when King Uther replied in his own voice, and without a halt in his speech: "It is my earnest wish and desire that Arthur wear my crown. I give him God's blessing and mine. I bid him therefore that he claim it, when the right time comes, in a righteous and just spirit. If he do not this thing he shall forfeit the blessing I now bestow on him."

The King had hardly finished these words when, with a sigh, his breath went from him and he died.

After the death of Uther, the kingdom was for a long time in great confusion, for every powerful noble wished to make himself king in the land.

Thus the barons strove, quarrelled, and made war on one another. But there dawned a day when they were as weary of themselves and their claims as the country was, and were not unwilling that from among them one should be chosen to be king.

Then Merlin went to the Archbishop of

Canterbury and advised him to ask all the lords of the kingdom and the gentlemen of arms to meet in London at Christmas, that they might make prayer to God that by some sign He should reveal the rightful King of the realm.

To London they came, in answer to the Archbishop's call; and many a knight had fasted first, and others had made clean their lives, that their prayers might be the better heard in Heaven.

On Christmas Day the lords gathered together, and with them the common people, a goodly company, either in St. Paul's or some other great church; and all men prayed long and earnestly that the sign should be given them which they asked for.

When the service was over they all passed out of the church and went into the church-yard, where they beheld a wonderful sight.

A great square stone lay there, and in the stone was an anvil, and through anvil and stone was a sword. About the sword were written in letters of gold these words: "He who pulleth this sword out of this stone and anvil is the rightly born King of England".

When all the lords saw these words they

tried, one after another, to pull the sword out of the stone. But no one was able to move it from its place. "He is not here," said the Archbishop, "who can draw out the sword. I do not doubt, however, but God will make him known. Let us appoint ten knights, men of good fame, to keep watch over the sword."

Then they agreed among themselves to meet on a future day, and to let any man who wished try his skill at withdrawing the sword. The Archbishop arranged that on New Year's Day there should be a tournament, and other fine doings, that the lords and commons should be kept together till the King should be revealed.

So upon New Year's Day the lords came together; and among them rode Sir Ector, a noble knight and one who had loved King Uther well, and in his company his son Sir Kay (who had received his knighthood but last Hallowmas), and young Arthur his adopted son, who was but a youth.

As they rode to the place of meeting, Sir Kay found that he had left his sword behind at their lodging, and he asked young Arthur to ride back and bring it for him.

"Right gladly will I do that," said the boy. "Haste you on with our father, I will return to the town with all speed and will bring your sword."

When he reached their lodging he knocked hard at the door, but no one answered, for they had all gone to the tournament.

Arthur was angry, and said to himself: "I will ride to the churchyard and take the sword from the stone, for I do not wish my brother to be without a sword this day."

When he came to the churchyard he alighted from his horse, and, going to the anvil, lightly pulled the sword out of the stone; and, mounting his horse again, he rode as fast as he could back to Sir Kay and gave him the sword.

Sir Kay grasped the sword, well pleased. His eye ran down it, and he knew it was the sword from the stone. He hastened to rejoin his father and tell him the news.

"Sir," cried he, when he came up to Sir Ector, "surely I, and none other, am chosen to be King of England, since in my hand I bear the sword of the stone!"

Sir Ector led his son and the boy Arthur into the church, and commanded his son to tell him truly how he had got the sword.

Sir Kay's face fell, but he answered stoutly: "My brother Arthur brought it to me."

Then said Sir Ector to Arthur, "Tell me, did you pluck the sword from the stone?"

Arthur at once confessed how, when he had reached home, he had found no one in the house to give him his brother's sword, so he had made all haste to the churchyard and plucked the sword from the stone that rested there.

"Were none there," asked Sir Ector, "to forbid the act?"

"Nay," said the boy, "they had gone, every one, to the tournament."

This was true, for the knights had gone to try their skill.

Then said Sir Ector to Arthur: "I know well you must be King of the land."

"Wherefore should I be King?" asked Arthur.

"Sir," was Ector's reply, "it is clearly ordained. For the man who can draw the sword out of the stone shall be rightful King of this land. Now, let me see if you can put the sword back in the stone and pull it out again."

"That is no hard task," said Arthur, and he put it back in the stone.

"My son, draw out the sword," said Sir Ector to Sir Kay.

And Sir Kay tried hard, bending down, the better to use his strength. Once he strove, and twice, but he could not withdraw the sword.

"Let me try," said Sir Ector; and, laying his hands upon the sword, he too strove to take it from the anvil and stone, but he could not move it from its place.

"Now you shall try again," said Sir Ector to Arthur; and when Arthur laid his hand upon the sword, it slid from the stone as a sunbeam across a wall. And when he had replaced it, it stuck as fast as before.

Then Sir Ector and Sir Kay knelt down upon the ground.

"Alas! my father and my brother," said Arthur, "why do you kneel to me?"

"By King Uther's wish you were entrusted to me," said Sir Ector to the boy. "I am not your father. You are of higher birth than I thought." Then he told him how Merlin had brought him to his good lady to be nurtured and brought up, till the time should come when he should receive his kingdom.

Arthur was very sorry when he heard that Sir Ector was not his father. But the knight cheered him up, and begged that when he be came King he would make Sir Kay steward of all his lands.

"That shall be done," said Arthur, "no man shall have that office but he."

And straightway they went to the Archbishop, who was struck with great wonder on hearing their story; but he advised that nothing should be said of the matter, since Twelfth Day was near at hand, when it would be given to every man to try his skill.

Now when Twelfth Day was come, all the barons gathered together for a trial with the sword. But none except Arthur was able to pull the sword out. Many of the lords were angry, and said it was a great shame that the kingdom should be governed by a boy of low birth.

The Archbishop said that the trial would be put off till Candlemas.

At Candlemas young Arthur again withdrew the sword, and no other could move it from its place. Wherefore the barons again began to quarrel, and demanded a new trial at Easter.

And at Easter the same thing happened, whereupon the matter was delayed till Pentecost.

At Pentecost the sword again was pulled

out by Arthur, and would yield itself to none other.

Then rose the commons, crying with one voice: "Arthur shall be our King! Hath not the sword revealed him to us, and the voice of God? We will have no other than he, and no further delay in the matter. And our prayer is that he will pardon us for what delay hath been. Those who stand up against him, we will slay." So they cried, bending their knees.

In this way was young Arthur proclaimed King of the realm of England, as revealed by God in answer to earnest prayer. The sword of the stone he laid upon the altar, and he was made the knight of the best man there.

Then the Archbishop took Arthur and crowned him King before them all, and Arthur swore unto his lords and commons that he would be a true king and do justly all the days of his life.

CHAPTER II

HOW ARTHUR GOT THE SWORD EXCALIBUR

ONE day King Arthur rode out with his wise man, Merlin. On the way he met King Pellinore, with whom he had a long and fierce fight. In the fight Arthur's sword was broken in two pieces. He received so many wounds that he had to stay for three days with a hermit. The hermit by his great skill healed his wounds.

So they continued their journey, and as they went along, the King said: "I have no sword."

"That does not matter," said Merlin, "for you will soon get another sword."

So they rode on till they came to a beautiful broad lake. King Arthur looked across its fair waters, and saw in the midst of the lake an arm rise out of the water. The arm was clothed in the whitest of soft silk, and the hand held aloft a beautiful sword.

"Lo," said Merlin, "there is the sword of which I spoke."

Thereupon they saw a beautiful maiden in a barge upon the lake.

"Who is the maiden?" said Arthur.

"She is the Lady of the Lake," said Merlin.

"There is a rock on the lake, and in it is a place as fair as any in the world. The maiden will soon come this way, and if you speak to her with fair words, she will give you that sword."

Quickly she drew near to them, and stepping lightly upon the shore, she saluted Arthur. He at once bowed before her.

"Maiden," said Arthur, "what sword is that which is held by the arm yonder above the water? I wish it were mine, for I have no sword."

"Sir King," said the maiden, "that sword is mine, and if you will give me a gift when I ask it of you, it shall be yours."

"By my faith," said Arthur, "I will give you whatever you ask for."

"Well," said the maiden, "step into the barge and row yourself to the sword. Take it with the scabbard, and when I see my time I will ask my gift."

Then King Arthur and Merlin dismounted from their horses and tied them to two trees. And entering the ship, they rowed out to the sword which was held above the water. King Arthur took it by the hilt, and the arm and hand sank below the surface again.

Then the two men came back once more to land, but nowhere could they see the maiden of the lake. So they mounted their horses and rode on.

King Arthur looked at the sword more closely, and he was well pleased with it.

"Which do you like better," said Merlin, "the sword or the scabbard?"

"I like the sword better," said Arthur.

"Then you are not wise," said Merlin, "for the sheath is worth more than ten swords. While you have the scabbard by your side, you will lose no blood, no matter how sorely you are wounded. I advise you, therefore, to keep the scabbard always with you." So they rode back to the King's palace.

CHAPTER III

THE MAIDEN AND THE SWORD

WHEN King Arthur was holding his Court at Camelot, there came to him a damsel who had been sent with a message from the great Lady Lille of Avalon. She wore a richly furred mantle; and when she let it fall from her shoulders, she was seen to be wearing a noble sword by her side.

The King marvelled when he saw this, and said: "Damsel, for what cause are you girt with that sword?"

"Sir," answered the maiden, "I do not wear this sword of my own free will. It is to me a cause of great sorrow, but no one can rid me of it except a knight, who not only must be a man strong to do great deeds, but whose heart also is free from all evil. If I can find such a knight, he will be able to draw the sword out of its sheath. I have been at the Court of King Ryons, for I was told that there were many good knights there. But neither he nor his knights were able to pull out the sword, though they all tried, one after the other."

"If this be true," said Arthur, "it is a wonderful thing. I will myself try to draw out the sword, not because I think I am the best knight, but because I wish to show an example to all the barons, that they also may make the attempt."

So the King took the sword by the sheath and the girdle and pulled eagerly at it, but it would not come out.

"Sir," said the damsel, "you need not pull at it half so hard, for the one that shall draw it forth will be able to do so quite easily."

"You are quite right," said Arthur. "So now, my barons, let each one of you make the attempt, but beware that you are not defiled with shame, treachery, or guile."

"It will be of no use," said the damsel, "for the one that pulls out the sword must be a pure knight and of noble birth, both on the father's and the mother's side."

Most of all the barons that were with Arthur at that time tried to draw out the sword, one after another; but after they had all done their best, the sword still remained in its sheath. Then the damsel was very sad at heart, and said: "Alas! I thought that at this Court I would find the best knights."

"By my faith," said Arthur, "I have here as good knights as any to be found in the whole world, but it appears that there is not one able to help you."

Now there was at that time a poor knight of Northumberland, who had been a prisoner for more than six months because he had slain King Arthur's cousin. He was called Balin the Savage. By the good graces of the barons he had just been let out of prison, and had come unawares into the Court.

He stood and watched the King and all his knights trying to draw the sword. But because he was poor, and shabbily dressed, he was ashamed to come forward, though he greatly desired to make the attempt.

The damsel was about to take her leave of Arthur and of all the barons, when Balin called unto her and said: "Damsel, I pray you of your courtesy to permit me to draw the sword if I can. Though I am so poorly clothed, yet I am a knight, and in my heart I feel as if I may be able to win success."

The damsel looked at the poor knight, and saw that he was a likely man as far as regards strength, but he was so poorly dressed that she could not think that he was a man of noble birth.

So she said: "Sir, it is no trouble; but it is hardly likely that you will succeed where so many great and noble knights have already failed."

"Ah! fair damsel," said Balin, "worthiness and good deeds are not in a man's clothing, but in him who wears it. Many a noble is not known by those around him."

"You speak the truth," said the damsel; "you can make the attempt to draw out the sword."

Then Balin took the sword by the girdle and the sheath, and drew forth the sword quite easily. When he looked at the sword, he was much pleased with it.

The King and all the barons wondered much that Balin should have been able to do what they could not, and some of the knights were very angry with Balin.

"Truly," said the damsel, "you are the best knight I have ever found, without any shame or treachery. You shall do many wonderful things yet. Now, gentle and courteous knight, give me back the sword again."

"Nay," said Balin, "for I will keep this sword till it is taken from me by force."

"Well," said the damsel, "you are not doing a wise thing in keeping the sword, for by it you will slay the best friend you have and the man you love most in the world. I warn you that the sword shall be the means of your own death."

Then Balin got his armour and horse, and made ready to depart from Camelot. The King begged him to stay at his Court, and he would do all in his power to make amends for the unkindness he had shown him. He promised also to advance him to high honour. Balin thanked the King for his kindness, but said that he must depart at once.

While Balin was making ready to go, there came into the Court the lady who was called the Lady of the Lake. She entered on horseback, richly dressed, and having saluted King Arthur, said that she had come to claim the gift he had promised her when she gave him the sword.

"That is true," said King Arthur; "I did promise you a gift, but I have forgotten the name of the sword that you gave me."

"The name of it," said the lady, "is Excalibur, that is to say, Cutsteel."

"Ask what you will," said King Arthur, "and you shall have it, if it lies in my power to give it."

"Well," said the lady, "I ask the head of that knight who hath won the sword, or else the head of the damsel who brought it. Though I have both their heads I shall still have sorrow, for the knight slew my brother, who was a good knight and true, and that damsel caused the death of my father."

"Truly," said King Arthur, "I cannot give you the head of either of them with honour; therefore ask what else you will, and I shall fulfil your desire."

"I shall ask nothing else," said the lady.

When Balin was just on the point of departing, he saw the Lady of the Lake. She had been the means of his mother's death, and he had searched for her everywhere for the last three years. When he was told that she had asked his head of King Arthur, he was very angry.

He went straight up to her, and in his anger said: "You would have my head, therefore you shall lose yours." And with his sword he smote off her head before King Arthur and all the Court.

Then the King was full of anger against Balin, and found fault with him very sharply. The knight told him that the lady had by her charms caused the deaths of many good knights, and that she had been the means of having his mother burned for witchery.

"Whatsoever cause of complaint you had against her," answered King Arthur sternly, "you should have kept back your hand in my presence. Such a thing was never done before at my Court. Therefore I advise you to leave my Court as soon as you can."

Then Balin took up the head of the lady and carried it with him to his inn. There he met his squire, and with him Balin rode forth out of the place, sorry at having made the King so angry.

CHAPTER IV

BALIN'S ADVENTURES

Now at that time there was at the Court a knight, the son of a king in Ireland, whose name was Sir Lanceor. He was very proud, and counted himself one of the best knights at the Court, and he felt very angry with Balin because he had won the sword. So he asked King Arthur if he would give him leave to ride after Balin and avenge the deed that he had done.

"Do your best," said Arthur; "I am very angry with Balin, and I wish him punished for what he has done to me and my Court."

Sir Lanceor went to his inn to prepare himself. He armed himself at all points, and put his shield on his shoulder. Having mounted his horse, he took his spear in his hand and rode after Balin as fast as his horse could go.

In a short time he came in sight of Balin, and with a loud voice he called upon him to stop. When Balin heard him, he turned his horse fiercely and asked Sir Lanceor if he wished to joust with him.

"Yes," answered the Irish knight, "for this reason have I come after you."

"Peradventure," said Balin, "it would have been better for you to stay at home, for many a man who thinks to rebuke his enemy rebukes himself. But from what Court do you come?"

"I am come from the Court of King Arthur," said the knight of Ireland, "to avenge the deed you have done to King Arthur and his Court."

"Well," said Balin, "I see well that I must fight you, though I do not wish to give further grief to King Arthur or any of his Court. Your quarrel is simple, for the lady I killed did much harm to me, or I would have been as unwilling as any knight that lives to take her life."

"Make you ready," said Sir Lanceor, "and let us meet, for one of us shall abide in the field."

Then they took their spears and rushed at one another as fast as their horses could carry them. The Irish knight broke his spear on

Balin's shield. But Balin gave him so great a thrust that he ran his spear through his shield and armour and pierced his body, so that he fell from his horse dead on the ground.

At first he did not know he had killed Sir Lanceor, as he had to turn his horse to draw out his spear. Then he saw Sir Lanceor lying on the ground.

Immediately after, a damsel came up as fast as her fair palfrey could ride. When she saw that Sir Lanceor was dead, she began to grieve for him beyond measure, for she had long loved him.

"Oh, Balin!" she said, "you have slain two bodies and one heart, and two hearts in one body." Thereupon she took the sword from Sir Lanceor as he lay on the ground and killed herself. At the sight of her Balin was very sad, and ashamed that so fair a damsel had slain herself for love of the dead knight.

At that moment Balin turned his horse away from the sad sight and looked toward a great forest. He saw another knight approaching, whom he knew from the arms he bore to be his brother Balan. They took off their helms and embraced one another.

Then Balan said: "I did not expect to meet

you here, but I am right glad to see you out of prison. A man told me in the castle of Four Stones that you had been set free, so I came hither, for here I thought I might perhaps find you."

Then Balin told his brother of his adventure of the sword, and of the death of the Lady of the Lake, and how King Arthur was displeased with him. He also told him how King Arthur had sent this knight after him, and that he had slain him, and how that the damsel on seeing him dead had killed herself.

As they talked together, there came riding past a king of Cornwall, called King Mark. When he saw the two dead bodies he asked how they had come by their deaths. When he heard how they had died, he was filled with pity that such true lovers had perished so sadly, and said: " I will not depart till I have in this place made a tomb." So he pitched his tent there, and sent his squires all round the country to find a tomb.

They found one that was fair and rich in a church, and brought it to the King. He then put the dead knight and lady in the tomb, and wrote on it the following inscription: " Here lieth Lanceor, the King's son of Ireland, that at his own request was slain by the hands of Balin; and his lady, Colombe, who slew herself with her lover's sword for grief and sorrow".

While King Mark was doing this, Merlin came and foretold that on this spot would be fought a great battle between the two bravest knights in the world. Then Merlin turned to Balin and said: "You have done yourself great harm because you did not save the lady who killed herself. Because of her death you shall strike the most dolorous stroke that ever man struck, for you shall hurt the truest knight that now lives, and on account of that stroke, three kingdoms shall be in great poverty and misery for twelve years, and the knight shall not be healed of the wound for many years."

Therewith Merlin vanished suddenly away, and Balin and his brother took leave of King Mark. Before leaving, King Mark wished to know Balin's name, but he did not tell it. So King Mark departed unto Camelot to King Arthur, and Balin and his brother took their way towards King Ryons.

As they rode along they again met Merlin, who told them what they were to do to secure King Ryons. They lodged that night in a wood among leaves, beside the highway. Having taken the bridles off their horses, they lay down to rest themselves.

About midnight Merlin bade them rise and make ready, for King Ryons was near at hand. The King had stolen away from his host with threescore horses of his best knights.

Anon Balin and his brother met with the King, and smote him from his horse, and wounded him badly. They slew also on the right hand and on the left more than forty of his men, and the rest fled. Then they went again to King Ryons, and would have slain him had he not yielded himself to them as a prisoner.

They laid him on a horse litter, for he was fiercely wounded. Merlin again vanished, and went to King Arthur at Camelot to tell him that his greatest enemy had been taken prisoner.

"By whom has he been taken?" said King Arthur.

"By two knights," said Merlin, "that would please your lordship, and to-morrow you shall know what knights they are."

Anon came Balin and Balan, and brought with them King Ryons. They delivered him to the porters and gave them charge of him. Then they set out on further adventures.

CHAPTER V

BALIN'S FIGHT WITH HIS BROTHER

WITHIN a day or two King Arthur was somewhat sick, and he had pitched his tent in a meadow and was lying therein on a pallet to sleep, but he could get no rest.

As he was lying there he heard a great noise, and on looking out of the tent he saw a knight pass, who was making great sorrow. When the King asked him the cause of his sorrow, he refused to tell it and passed on.

Then came Balin, who, when he saw King Arthur, alighted from his horse and came to the King on foot, and saluted him. The King asked him to go after the knight and make him return, either by force or of his own free will.

This Balin readily agreed to do, and rode after the Knight, whom he found with a damsel in a forest. "Sir Knight," said Balin, "you must return with me unto King Arthur to tell him of your sorrow." But the knight refused, saying that it was of no use.

"Sir," said Balin, "I pray you make ready, for you must go with me, or else I must fight with you and bring you by force."

"Will you be my warrant," said the knight, "and I will go with you." Balin said he was willing to undertake this, so the knight returned with Balin, and the damsel was left behind.

Just as they reached the King's tent, suddenly there came one who was invisible and smote the knight that came with Balin through the body with a spear.

"Alas!" said the knight, "I am slain under your conduct by a knight called Garlon. Therefore take my horse, that is better than yours, and ride to the damsel, and follow the quest that I was in, wherever she will lead you, and avenge my death when you may."

This Balin agreed to do, and departed from the knight with great sorrow. King Arthur caused the knight to be honourably buried.

Then Balin and the maiden rode three or four days without any adventure, but in the evening of the fourth day they came to the castle of a rich gentleman. As they sat at supper Balin heard someone crying at his side, and he asked what was wrong.

"I will tell you," said his host. "I was lately at a tournament, and jousted twice with a knight, who is brother to King Pellam, and twice I smote him down. Then he promised

to have revenge on my best friend, so he
wounded my son, who cannot be cured till I
have that knight's blood. He rides always
invisible, but I do not know his name."

"Ah!" said Balin, "I know that knight. His
name is Garlon, and he has slain two knights
of mine in the same way. I had rather meet
that knight than have all the gold in this
realm."

His host told him that King Pellam of Listeneise had arranged to hold a great feast that
would last twenty days, and that if they went
hither they would see his brother Garlon.

On the morn they all three rode toward Pellam, and they had a journey of fifteen days
before they reached the city of Listeneise. On
the day of their arrival the great feast began.
Having alighted from their horses, they went
into the castle. Balin's host, however, did not
enter.

Balin was well received, and led to a chamber, where he took off his armour. There were
brought to him rich robes, and the squires would
have taken his sword from him. But Balin
refused to leave his sword behind, saying it
was the custom for a knight in his country
always to keep his sword by his side.

So he was allowed to wear his sword. Then he went into the great hall with the lady, and was set among the knights. Soon Balin asked a knight if there was not one at this Court called Garlon.

"Yonder he is," said the knight of whom he asked the question, "he with the dark face. He is the most wonderful knight now living, for he destroys many good knights, as he goes invisible."

Balin considered for a long time what he ought to do, and kept gazing at Garlon. But Garlon, when he saw Balin looking at him so earnestly, went up to him and smote him on the face with the back of his hand, saying: "Knight, why do you look at me so? For shame! Eat your food, and do what you came for."

"You say well," said Balin. "This is not the first wrong you have done me, and therefore will I do that for which I came hither." At once he rose up and clave Garlon's head to the shoulders. Then Balin called unto the knight who had brought him to Listeneise, saying: "Now you may get blood enough to heal your son's wound with."

All the knights rose from the table to set on Balin, and King Pellam himself rose up fiercely and cried: "Knight, have you slain my brother? For this deed you shall die before you depart."

"Well," said Balin, "do it yourself."

"Yes," said Pellam, "no other man but myself shall do it, for my brother's sake."

Then King Pellam caught up a heavy weapon and smote eagerly at Balin. But Balin put his sword between the stroke and his head, with the result that his sword was broken to pieces. When Balin had thus lost his sword he ran from room to room seeking for a weapon, but could find none. Pellam followed after him.

At last Balin came to a room that was richly furnished; and in it stood a bed arrayed with cloth of gold, the richest that could be thought of. By the bed stood a table of pure gold, with four pillars of silver, and on the table was a marvellous spear, strangely wrought.

When Balin saw the spear he took it in his hand and turned on King Pellam. He struck him so hard that King Pellam fell down in a swoon.

Thereupon the castle roof and walls broke and tumbled to the earth, and Balin also fell, so that he might not stir hand or foot. And now Balin had struck the dolorous stroke which had been foretold by Merlin, and for three days he lay insensible.

Then Merlin came thither, and he took up Balin and got him a good horse, and bade him ride out of that country. Balin wished to take with him the damsel, but Merlin told him she was dead. For twelve years King Pellam suffered severely from the wound Balin had given him, for it could not be healed till Galahad, the good knight, would do so during the quest of the Holy Grail. Three countries were also reduced to great misery by the dolorous stroke.

When Balin was out of these countries he came to a cross, whereon were written in letters of gold: "It is not for any knight alone to ride towards this castle". Then he saw an old white-haired gentleman coming towards him that said: "Balin the Savage, you pass your bounds to come this way, therefore turn again, and it will avail you."

With this the old gentleman vanished away, and Balin heard a horn blow as if for the death of a beast in the chase. "That blast," said Balin, "is blown for me, for I am the prize, and yet I am not dead."

Then he saw a hundred ladies and many

knights, who welcomed him with great joy and led him into the castle, where there was dancing and playing.

The chief lady of the castle said to Balin: "Knight of the two swords, you must joust with the knight that keeps the island close by, for no man can pass this way but he must joust before he goes farther."

"That is an unhappy custom," said Balin: "that a knight may not pass this way unless he joust. Well, since it is my duty, I am ready. But travelling men are often weary, and their horses too. But though my horse is weary, my heart is not weary. But I should be little sorry if I were to die here."

"Sir," said one of the knights of the castle, "your shield is not good, I will lend you a bigger one." So he took the shield that was unknown, and left his own at the castle. He rode to the island and put himself and his horse into a great boat.

When he came to the other side he met a damsel, and she said: "Oh, Knight Balin, why have you left your own shield? Alas! you have put yourself in great danger, for by your shield you should have been known."

"I am sorry," said Balin, "that I ever came

to this country, but I may not turn back again for shame. I will take the adventure that comes to me, be it life or death."

Before him he saw come riding out of the castle a knight in red armour, and his horse was dressed in the same colour. When this knight saw Balin he thought he was like his brother, because of the two swords. But because he knew not his shield, he thought it was not he.

So the two brothers ran together with such force that both were unhorsed. Balin was sore bruised with the fall of his horse, for he was weary with travel. Balan was the first to rise to his feet. He drew his sword and advanced to meet Balin, who also rose and prepared for the attack.

But Balan smote Balin first, striking through his shield and cleaving his helm. Then Balin smote him in return with that unhappy sword, and the blow nearly felled his brother. For a long time they fought, till they were both out of breath.

Then Balin looked up to the castle and saw the towers full of ladies. So they went at the battle again, and wounded one another grievously. Often they had to stop for want of breath.   At last Balan, the younger brother, withdrew a little, and lay down on the ground.

Balin the Savage went forward to him and said: "What knight are you?   For before this time I have never found a knight that matched me as you have done."

"My name," said he, "is Balan, brother to the good knight Balin."

"Alas!" said Balin, "that ever I should see this day."   Thereupon he fell back in a swoon. Then Balin crept on all-fours to him and unloosed his helmet, and found that it was his brother.   When Balin came to himself, he said: "Oh, Balan, my brother, you have slain me, and I you, wherefore all the wide world shall speak of us both."

"Alas!" said Balan, "that I ever saw this day, that through mishap I might not know you.   I knew well your two swords, but because of the strange shield I thought you were another knight."

"All this was caused by an unhappy knight in the castle, for he made me leave my own shield, which has caused both our deaths.   I would that I could live to destroy that castle for its evil customs."

Then Balan died, and at midnight after

Balin died. They were buried together, and the lady of the castle had Balan's name written on the tomb, and how he was there slain by his brother's hands, but she did not know Balin's name.

On the morrow came Merlin and wrote Balin's inscription on the tomb in letters of gold: "Here lieth Balin the Savage, who was the knight with the two swords, and who smote the dolorous stroke".

Soon after this, Merlin came to King Arthur and told him of the dolorous stroke that Balin gave to King Pellam, and how Balin and Balan fought together the most marvellous battle that ever was heard of, and how they were buried together in one tomb.

"Alas!" said King Arthur, "this is the greatest pity that I ever heard tell of, for in the world I know not two such knights."

Thus endeth the tale of Balin and Balan, two brethren born in Northumberland, good knights.

CHAPTER VI

KING ARTHUR AND THE GIANT

AT one time King Arthur, having left his Queen and realm in the hands of Sir Baudwin and Constantine during his absence from the country, set sail from Sandwich with a great army in many ships, and sailed away to Flanders.

And as the King lay in his cabin, he fell asleep and dreamed a wonderful dream. He seemed to see in his dream a dreadful dragon come flying out of the west and drown many of his soldiers. Its head was of a deep-blue; its shoulders appeared to shine like burnished gold; its body was covered with scales of a wonderful colour; its tail was like a whip with many lashes; its claws were like unto fine gold; and out of its mouth came a fiery flame.

Then there seemed to come out of the east a fierce black boar, with legs as big as posts. He roared so loudly that it was terrible to hear him. The dragon attacked the boar with great fury, while the boar with his sharp tusks ran at the dragon and so badly wounded him that all the sea round about became red with blood.

The dragon thereupon raised himself on high and came down with such force on the boar that he ground him all to powder, both flesh and bones, and the powder was scattered by the wind far and wide over sea and land.

Then the King awoke, and was much puzzled to know what the dream meant. So he sent for Merlin and asked him what was its meaning.

"Sir," said the wise man, "the dragon that you dreamed about is your own self, and the colours of his wings are the realms you have won, and the tail with the whip-like lashes represents the noble knights of the Round Table. The boar is some tyrant or giant that you are to overcome. Therefore have no doubt or fear as to your success."

After this they came in sight of land, and before long they arrived at Flanders. Then there came to the King a man of that country and told him that a great giant had devoured many people belonging to that district. For seven long years he had destroyed the children of that people, so that now there were no children left.

"Lately," said the countryman, "he has taken captive the Duchess of Brittany as she was riding through the land with her servants, and has carried her off to his mountain cave. More than five hundred of her followers have attempted to rescue her, but without success. She was the wife of your cousin, Sir Howel. Now as you are the rightful king of this land, have pity upon her and us, and deliver us from the great monster."

"Now," said King Arthur, "can you lead me to the place where this giant has his den?"

"Yes, I can, sir," said the man. "Yonder you can see two great fires up the side of the mountain. Near them you will find the giant's cave, and in it, I believe, more treasure than is to be found in the whole of France."

When the King had heard these words he returned to his tent. Then he sent for Sir Kay and another knight, Sir Bedivere by name. When they came into his presence, he gave them orders to make ready secretly horses and armour for himself and them, for he intended to take them with him to the mountain called St. Michael's Mount. He immediately got himself ready and armed himself at all points. The two knights did the same. Then they all three rode as fast as they could, till they came to the foot of the mountain.

There they dismounted from their horses. "Stay here," said the King, "for I will go alone up the mountain." Then he ascended the hill till he came to a great fire. There he found a widow, sitting by the side of a newly-made grave. She was wringing her hands and making great sorrow. The King saluted her, and asked her the reason of her great grief.

"Speak gently, Sir Knight," she said in a low voice, "for yonder is a monster who, if he hears you, will come and destroy you. You are most unlucky. Why did you come to this mountain? If there were fifty men as brave as you are, you would not be able to conquer the giant. Here in this grave lies my mistress, the Duchess of Brittany, wife of Sir Howel, who has met her death at his hands."

"I am come," said the King, "from King Arthur himself, to rid the earth of this tyrant."

"But he does not heed either king or any man," said the woman. "Do not go too near him, for he has already conquered fifteen kings. If you still desire to speak with him, meet him at the great fire at supper-time."

King Arthur then told her that, notwithstanding her words, he meant to do that for which he had come.   So he strode to the top of the hill, where he saw the giant sitting at his supper.   He was indeed fearful to look upon.

The King was greatly vexed at the sight, and going boldly forward he addressed the giant in these words: "Why have you slain these innocent children and put to death this Duchess? Arise, prepare yourself for fight, for this day you shall die at my hand!"

The giant at once sprang to his feet and laid hold of his great club.   Then he rushed at King Arthur and aimed at his head with the club, but the blow fell only on the crest of his helmet, which was broken off.   The King, however, returned the blow again and again.

The giant then threw away his club and caught the King in his arms.   So strong was the giant's grip that the King was sorely crushed.   The struggle became so fierce that, at last, the two, still holding on to one another, rolled down the slope of the hill to the edge of the sea.   There they were seen by Sir Kay and Sir Bedivere, but before the two knights came to his aid, the King had given the giant his deathblow.   The two knights now released the King from the giant's grip.

The King then commanded Sir Kay to cut off the giant's head and bear it to Sir Howel, that he might know that his enemy was dead. Afterwards the head of the giant was to be fixed to a gate, so that the people of these parts might no longer fear the giant.

Then King Arthur said to Sir Kay and Sir Bedivere: "Go up to the mountain and fetch me my shield, my sword, and the club of iron. As for the treasure, take it for yourselves. You will find plenty of it. I desire no more than the giant's club."

The knights did as they were ordered, and they all returned to the army. When the people knew what had taken place, they came and thanked the King. But he said: "Nay, rather give the thanks to God for His deliverance." And he commanded his cousin Howel to build a church on the mountain in the name of Saint Michael.

CHAPTER VII

SIR LAUNCELOT OF THE LAKE

Soon after King Arthur had returned from Rome to England, all the knights of the

Round Table came to the Court. Day by day they engaged in all kinds of knightly exercises, and many of them gained still greater honour and renown. But of all the knights, Sir Launcelot of the Lake was especially famous for his deeds of arms, both for death and life. So he is the first knight that the French book, from which this story is taken, speaks of after King Arthur came from Rome.

Queen Guinevere esteemed him above all other knights; and in return he was devoted to her beyond all other ladies and damsels all his life. On her account he did many deeds of arms, and on one occasion by his bravery saved her from the fire.

Like all the knights of the Round Table, Sir Launcelot wished to prove himself a true knight in wild and strange adventures, so along with his nephew, Sir Lionel, he mounted his horse one day and rode away from the palace.

After going some distance they came to a forest. Here Sir Launcelot lay down to rest, and soon fell fast asleep. While he slept, Sir Lionel was defeated by a strong knight, who bound him fast and rode with him to his own castle. The name of this knight was Sir Turquine.

Sir Launcelot was found by four queens in the forest as he slept. One of them, Morgan Le Fay, put an enchantment upon him, by which he would not awake for six hours. Then they took him into her castle. He was, however, set free by a damsel, who as a reward made him promise that he would assist her father on the following week in his fight with the King of North Wales.

So Sir Launcelot escaped from the castle, and came to the same forest in which he had fallen asleep. He was told that it belonged to Sir Turquine, and that it was near his castle, in which he had put no fewer than threescore and four of King Arthur's good knights. Among these were Sir Lionel and Sir Ector, the foster-father of Arthur.

He saw coming through the forest Sir Turquine, carrying a wounded knight bound across his horse. This was Sir Gaheris, Gawaine's brother, a knight of the Round Table.

Sir Launcelot at once rode up to him, and asked him to put down the wounded knight and prepare to fight him. After a long and fierce struggle Sir Turquine was slain, and Sir

Launcelot ordered Sir Gaheris to ride to the castle and deliver all the knights.

Sir Launcelot now went with the damsel on his way. "Sir," said the lady, "not far from here hides a knight who is a terror to all ladies and robs them."

"What," said Sir Launcelot, "is he a thief and a knight? He is a shame to the name of knighthood. It is a pity that he is allowed to live. But ride you on yourself in front, and I will hide myself. If he troubles you, I shall come to your rescue."

So the maid rode on at a gentle pace. And in a short time the knight came out from the wood and dragged the damsel from her horse. Then came Sir Launcelot as fast as he could ride, and struck the knight such a blow on the helmet with his sword that he lay on the ground dead.

"Now you have the payment that you have so long deserved," said Sir Launcelot, addressing the dead knight.

"That is true," replied the damsel, "for he has for a long time been a cause of distress to ladies."

"Now, maiden," said Sir Launcelot, "can I be of any further service to you?"

"Nay, sir, not at this time," she answered. "And for your kindness may God preserve you wherever you go!"

Sir Launcelot now took his leave of the maiden, and rode through a deep forest for two days.

On the third day he came to a long bridge. As he was riding across it, there suddenly started upon him a rough churl, who struck at the nose of the knight's horse so that it turned about.

"Why do you ride across this bridge without leave?" asked the man.

"Why should I not ride?" said Sir Launcelot. "It is the way I choose to ride."

"You shall not choose," said the churl, and struck at him with a great club shod with iron.

Then Sir Launcelot drew his sword and soon put an end to this man.

At the end of the bridge was a fair village, and all the people warned him of his danger, but he rode straight up to the castle. When he came there, he alighted from his horse and tied it to a ring in the wall. He saw a beautiful green courtyard, and round about it the doors and windows were open. A number of people were looking out, and they cried: "Fair knight, you are unfortunate."

Then there came against him two great giants, well armed except as regards their heads, and with horrible clubs in their hands. Sir Launcelot put his shield before him, and, having parried the stroke of the one giant, he clove his head with his sword. When the other saw what had taken place, he ran away for fear of the terrible strokes. But Sir Launcelot rushed after him and put him to death.

Then the victor entered the hall, and there came before him threescore gentlewomen, who knelt and thanked God and the knight for setting them free.

"Sir," said they, "the most of us have been here seven years as prisoners of the two giants, who have kept us working all kinds of silk works for our food. We all pray you to tell us your name, that we may make known to our friends who it was that delivered us out of prison."

"Fair ladies," said the knight, "my name is Sir Launcelot of the Lake. You can tell your friends how and by whom you were delivered. And if I happen to come to any of your lands, I trust you will show me good cheer. What treasure there is in this castle, I give it to you to make up for what you have suffered."

Then he mounted his horse again, and went on his way as before.

One night Sir Launcelot came to the court-yard of an old gentleman, who lodged him with a good will, and gave him plenty of food both for himself and his horse.

When it was time to retire for the night, the host took him to a fair garret over the gate. There Sir Launcelot unarmed himself and set his armour beside him, and went to bed, where he soon fell asleep.

Soon afterwards there came a knight on horseback, and in great haste knocked at the gate. When Sir Launcelot heard the knocking, he rose up and looked out of the window, and saw by the light of the moon that three knights were pursuing that one man. All three attacked him at once with their swords, but he turned on them and defended himself as became a knight.

"Truly," said Sir Launcelot, "I shall help yonder one knight, for I am ashamed to see three knights attack one. If he is slain, I am to a certain extent to blame for his death."

So he put on his armour and let himself down from the window by a sheet.

"Turn your swords against me," said Sir Launcelot to the three knights, "and leave off fighting with that knight."

They all three left Sir Kay, for it was he that the three knights had attacked, and turned to Sir Launcelot. Then began a furious battle, for the three of them got off their horses and assailed Sir Launcelot on every side.

Sir Kay prepared to assist Sir Launcelot, but he cried out: "Nay, sir, I will have none of your help, so if you wish me to aid you, leave me to fight alone."

Sir Kay agreed to the request and stood aside: Sir Launcelot within six strokes had struck all three to the ground.

At once they all cried out: "Sir Knight, we yield to you as a man of might." But Sir Launcelot made them yield to Sir Kay, and only on that condition would he spare their lives.

At first they were not very willing to do so, but Sir Launcelot was firm, and in the end they accepted his condition. "Fair knight," they said, "since you have spared our lives, we will do as you command us."

They also promised to go next Whitsunday to the Court of King Arthur, and to yield themselves as prisoners to Queen Guinevere.

So Sir Launcelot suffered them to depart, and then he knocked at the gate with the pommel of his sword. The host came, and Sir Kay and he entered the house.

"Sir," said the host, "I thought you were in bed."

"So I was," said Sir Launcelot, "but I got up and leapt out of the window to help an old companion of mine."

When they came into the light, Sir Kay recognized Sir Launcelot, and at once kneeled down and thanked him for his kindness in thus saving his life.

"Sir," said Sir Launcelot, "I have done nothing but what I ought to do, and you are welcome, and shall stay here and rest yourself."

When Sir Kay had taken off his armour, he asked for food, which was brought, and he had a good supper. When he had finished they both went to bed, the knights sharing the same bed.

In the morning Sir Launcelot rose early, and left Sir Kay sleeping. He put on Sir Kay's armour and took his shield. He next went to the stable, where he got Sir Kay's horse, and having taken leave of his host, he went in search of further adventures.

Soon afterwards Sir Kay arose. He missed Sir Launcelot, and then he saw that his armour and horse had been taken. "Now, by my faith," he said, "I know well that he will grieve some of the Court of King Arthur, for he will draw on him the attack of some knights. They will think it is I, and will on that account be all the bolder against him. But since I have his armour and shield I shall ride in peace." Then soon after, Sir Kay thanked his host and departed.

After Sir Launcelot had ridden for some time through a great forest, he came to a piece of flat country full of rivers and meadows. In front of him he saw a long bridge, on which stood three beautifully furnished tents.

Outside of the tents there hung three white shields, and at the door of each of the tents stood three squires. Sir Launcelot, however, passed by the tents and said not a word. When he was past, the three knights said to one another that it was the proud Sir Kay. "He thinks," said they, "there is no knight so good as he, but it has been proved that this is not always the case."

"By my faith," said one of the knights, Sir Gaunter by name, "I will ride after him and try my skill against him.   You will see how I fare."

So Sir Gaunter put on his armour and hung his shield on his shoulder. When he had mounted his horse, a squire gave him his spear, and he galloped after Sir Launcelot.

When he came up to him, he cried out: "Stay, proud Sir Kay, you shall not pass this way without my leave."

Sir Launcelot at once turned round, and the two knights rushed at one another with all their might. Sir Gaunter's spear was broken, and Sir Launcelot smote him and his horse to the ground.

When Sir Gaunter had fallen, the other two knights said one to the other: "Yonder knight is not Sir Kay, for he is taller than Sir Kay."

"I am sure," said Sir Gilmere, "yon knight has slain Sir Kay and taken his horse and armour."

"Whether this be so or not," said Sir Raynold, the third knight, "let us now mount our horses and go to the aid of Sir Gaunter. We shall have work enough to match that knight, for it appears to me to be either Sir Launcelot, or Sir Tristram, or Sir Pelleas, the good knight."

Then they mounted their horses and rode after Sir Launcelot. When they overtook him, Sir Gilmere rushed at him with his spear, but Sir Launcelot smote him so that he lay on the ground as if he were dead.

"Sir Knight," said Sir Raynold, "you are a strong man, and as you have slain my two brethren, my heart is sore against you. If I could with honour leave you alone, I would do so. But I must fight against you as they have done. Therefore, Sir Knight, make ready!"

The two knights attacked one another with great force, and both their spears were broken. Then they both drew their swords and continued the fight.

Sir Gaunter now recovered himself, and going over to where Sir Gilmere lay, he ordered him to get up and go with him to the assistance of Sir Raynold. Thereupon they leapt on their horses and made a furious attack on Sir Launcelot.

When Sir Launcelot saw them coming, he struck at Sir Raynold with his sword with such force, that he fell off his horse to the ground. Then he struck at the other two knights, and with two strokes unhorsed them.

Sir Raynold, covered with blood, now got

up, and once again made straight for Sir Launcelot.

"Now let be," said Sir Launcelot; "I was not far from you when you were made a knight, Sir Raynold. I know you are a good knight, and I am unwilling to slay you."

When Sir Raynold saw it was Sir Launcelot, he said: "I dare say both my brethren and I will not be unwilling to yield to you if we knew who you were. We know well that you are not Sir Kay."

"You shall go on Whitsunday and yield yourselves as prisoners to Queen Guinevere, and say that Sir Kay sent you."

They agreed to do Sir Launcelot's commands. So Sir Launcelot departed, and the knights gave one another all the help they could.

CHAPTER VIII

SIR GALAHAD

At the vigil of Pentecost, when all the knights of the Round Table were come to Camelot and the tables were set ready for food, a fair gentlewoman entered the hall. She had ridden so

fast that her horse was all covered with sweat.
Having alighted from her horse, she appeared
before the King and saluted him.

"Sire," she said, "tell me where Sir Launcelot is."

"Yonder he is," said the King, pointing to
Sir Launcelot, who stood at a little distance
from the King.

Then she went up to Sir Launcelot and said:
"Sir Launcelot, in the name of King Pelles
I salute you, and I wish you to come with
me into a forest."

Sir Launcelot asked her where she stayed.
She told him that she dwelt with King Pelles
and on his asking her what she wanted
with him, she said he would find out when
he reached the castle of King Pelles. Sir
Launcelot gladly agreed to go with her.

He bade his squire saddle his horse and
bring his armour. This was done with all
haste. The Queen on seeing Sir Launcelot
ready to leave Camelot, asked him if he was
going to depart from the feast. The gentlewoman replied on his behalf, saying: "Madam,
he shall be back again to-morrow by dinner-
time."

So Sir Launcelot departed with the gentlewoman, and rode until he came into a great valley. There they saw an abbey of nuns. The gates being opened, they entered, and alighted from their horses. A number of people came out to welcome him, and were very glad of his coming.

When they had led him into the abbey he found two of his cousins there, Sir Bors and Sir Lionel. They were delighted to see him, and enquired of him the reason of his coming. They had expected to see him next day at Camelot.

While they were still talking, there came twelve nuns, who brought with them Galahad. He was passing fair and well made, so that in the world men could hardly find his equal.

"Sir," said the nuns, "we bring you here this child, whom we have nourished. We pray you to make him a knight, for he may not receive the order of knighthood from worthier hands."

Sir Launcelot beheld the young squire, and saw that he was seemly, and yet demure as a dove. He thought he had never seen a man at his age so fair of form. Then Sir Launcelot said to the nuns: " Does this desire come of himself?"

He and all of them said: "Yea."

"Then shall he," said Sir Launcelot, "receive the order of knighthood to-morrow."

That night Sir Launcelot was well entertained, and on the morrow at an early hour, at Galahad's desire, he made him a knight, saying: "God make you a good man, for you are more beautiful than any other man." Sir Launcelot then asked the young knight to go with him to the Court of King Arthur, but he said he would not go at this time.

Then Sir Launcelot departed from the abbey, taking with him his two cousins, and they came to Camelot before nine o'clock on Whitsunday morning. By that time the King and Queen had gone to the minster to service.

When they came back, they were very glad to see Sir Launcelot and his cousins. As they entered the hall, each of the barons sought for his name, written with golden letters, in the seats of the Round Table.

They went from seat to seat till they came to the Siege Perilous, where they found letters newly written in gold, that said: "Four hundred and fifty-four winters after the passion of our Lord Jesus Christ ought this seat to be filled".

They all thought it a wonderful thing to see

this writing. Then Sir Launcelot reckoned the time of the writing from the birth of our Lord unto that day, and said: "It seems to me this seat ought to be filled to-day, for this is the Feast of Pentecost after four hundred and fifty-four years. If it pleases all parties, I would like none of these letters to be seen to-day, till he comes who ought to achieve this adventure."

Orders were given to cover the letters in the Siege Perilous with a cloth of silk, and the King made haste to go in to dinner.

"Sir," said Sir Kay the Steward, "if you now go to meat, you shall break your old custom, for it has not been usual to sit down to meat on this day until you have seen some adventure."

"You speak the truth," said the King; "but I was so delighted to see Sir Launcelot and his cousins safe back, that I forgot all about my old custom."

As they stood speaking, a squire came in and said to the King: "Sir, I bring wonderful tidings. Beneath at the river I saw a great stone floating above the water, and in it a sword."

So the King and his knights went down to

the river, and there they saw a stone floating, as it were of red marble, with a fair rich sword stuck in it. In the handle of it were precious stones wrought with gold.

Then the barons read the letters, which were as follow: "Never shall man take me hence but only he by whose side I ought to hang, and he shall be the best knight in the world".

When the King had seen the letters, he said unto Sir Launcelot: "Fair sir, this sword ought to be yours, for I am sure you are the best knight in the world."

Then Sir Launcelot replied: "Sir, it is not my sword. You know well that I have not the hardihood to set my hand to it, for it does not belong to my side. Also, who assays to take the sword and fails, shall receive a wound by that sword that he shall not recover of for a long time. This day shall the adventures of the Holy Grail begin."

"Now, fair nephew," said the King unto Sir Gawaine, "assay you to take the sword." Sir Gawaine was at first unwilling, but the King commanded him to do so. He took up the sword by the handles, but he was unable to move it.

"My Lord Sir Gawaine." said Sir Launcelot,

"do you not know that this sword will wound you so much, that you will wish you had never touched it?"

Then the King said unto Sir Percivale that he should try to move the sword. So he set his hand to the sword and drew it strongly, but he was not able to move it either. Then a few more of the barons tried to move the sword, but they all failed.

"Now may you go to your dinner," said Sir Kay to the King, "for you have seen a wonderful adventure." So the King and all the knights went in to dinner, every knight knew his own place and took his own seat.

When all the seats were filled except the Siege Perilous, a wonderful thing happened. All the doors and windows of the palace shut of themselves. Yet the hall was not greatly darkened, and they were all amazed. Then King Arthur stood up and said: "Fair knights, we have seen marvels to-day, but before night I suppose we shall see greater marvels."

As they sat there, an old man came in, clothed all in white, and no knight knew where he had come from. With him he brought a young knight on foot, with red armour, but without sword or shield, save a scabbard hanging by his side. Then the old man said unto King Arthur: "Sir, I bring here a young knight, who is descended from kings and is of the kindred of Joseph of Arimathea, and by him the marvels of this Court and of strange realms shall be fully accomplished."

The King was very pleased to hear the old man's words, and bade him and the young knight welcome. Then the old man made the young man take off his armour. He was in a coat of red silk, and bore a mantle upon his shoulder, that was furred with ermine.

Then the old knight led him to the Siege Perilous, beside which sat Sir Launcelot. The good man lifted up the cloth and saw there the letters that said thus: "This is the siege of Galahad, the high prince". He set him down in it, saying: "This place is yours."

The young knight then said to the old man: "Sir, you may now go your way, and tell King Pelles that I shall come and see him as soon as ever I am able."

So the good man departed, and having met twenty noble squires, he went back to King Pelles.

All the knights of the Round Table were greatly surprised that Sir Galahad dared sit in that Siege Perilous, as he was so young. They did not know where he had come from. "This is he," said they, "by whom the Holy Grail shall be achieved."

Then Sir Launcelot beheld his son and was greatly rejoiced. So great was the noise in all the Court that it came to the ears of the Queen. She wondered what knight it was that dared sit in the Siege Perilous. Many told the Queen that he greatly resembled Sir Launcelot. "I should like to see him," said the Queen, "for he must needs be a noble man, for his father is one."

When the King and all the knights had risen from the table, the King went to the Siege Perilous and lifted up the cloth. There he found the name of Galahad. He showed it to Sir Gawaine and said: "Fair nephew, now we have among us Sir Galahad, who shall achieve the Holy Grail."

Then he turned to Galahad and bade him welcome to the Court. "Sir, you are welcome," he said, "for you shall move many knights to the quest of the Holy Grail, and you shall accomplish that which many knights have failed to do."

He took him by the hand and went down

from the palace to show Galahad the adventures of the stone. "Sir," said the King to him, "here is as great a marvel as ever I saw, and right good knights have assayed and failed."

"Sir," said Sir Galahad, "that is no marvel, for this adventure is not theirs but mine, and I was so sure of this sword that I brought none with me; for here by my side hangs the scabbard."

He then laid his hand on the sword and lightly drew it out of the stone and put it in the sheath, and said to the King: "Now it goes better than it did before."

"Sir," said the King, "God shall send you a shield."

Sir Galahad was unwilling, however, to take any shield from the King.

The King and all the estates went home unto Camelot, and at evensong went to the great minster. After that they went to supper, and every knight sat in his own place at the Round Table. Whilst they sat at supper, they heard cracking and noise of thunder that should, as it appeared to them, shake the place all to pieces. In the midst of this blast entered a sunbeam seven times clearer than they ever saw in the daytime. They were all alighted of the grace of the Holy Ghost.

Then the knights looked upon one another and saw each other fairer than they had ever seen in their lives before. There was no knight might speak a word for a long time, and so they looked every man on his fellows, as if they were dumb.

Then there entered into the hall the Holy Grail, covered with white silk, but no one could see it or who bore it. All the hall was filled with good odours, and every knight had such food and drink as he loved best in this world. When the Holy Grail had been borne through the hall, it departed suddenly so that they did not know what had become of it.

Then they had all breath to speak. And the King gave thanks to God for the good grace that He had sent them. "We ought to thank our Lord Jesus greatly," said the King, "for what He has shown us to-day at the feast of Pentecost."

"Now," said Sir Gawaine, "we have been greatly blessed to-day, but one thing escaped us—we did not see the Holy Grail, it was so preciously covered. Wherefore I will here make a vow that without further delay I shall labour in the quest of the Holy Grail for a twelvemonth and a day, or more if need be. I shall not return unto the Court till I have seen it more openly than it has been seen here to-day. If I do not speed in my quest, I shall return again."

When the knights of the Round Table heard these words of Sir Gawaine's, a great number arose and made the same vows. When King Arthur heard this, he was greatly vexed, for he knew well that they would not break their vows, and he should be bereft of the fairest and truest knights that ever were seen together in any part of the world. For when they departed from Camelot, he was sure they would never all meet again in this world, for many should die in the quest.

The Queen and the ladies of the Court were also grieved when they heard the tidings. Many of the ladies would have gone with the knights, had not an old man in religious clothing said that the knights were to go alone. He warned them that any knight that was not clean of his sins would not see the Holy Grail.

Then they went to rest themselves. In honour of the greatness of Galahad he was led into King Arthur's chamber, and there rested in his own bed. As soon as it was day the King arose, for he had had no rest all night for sorrow. Then the King and Queen went to the minster, and all the knights in full armour save their shields and helms followed them to hear the service.

After service was over, the King wished to know how many knights had undertaken the quest of the Holy Grail. They found there were a hundred and fifty, and all were knights of the Round Table. Then they put on their helms and mounted their horses, and rode through the street of Camelot. There was weeping of rich and poor, and the King turned away and could not speak for tears.

A short time after, they came to a city and a castle called Vagon. The lord of the castle was a good man, and set open the gates and heartily welcomed them to his home. On the morrow they all departed, each knight taking the way he liked best.

Now Sir Galahad was yet without a shield, and he rode four days without meeting any adventure. After evensong on the fourth day he came to a white abbey, where he was treated with great kindness. On being taken

into a room he found there two knights of
the Round Table, Sir Bagdemagus and Sir
Uwaine.

"Sirs," said Galahad, "what adventure
brought you to this place?" They told him
that within the abbey was a shield that no
man could bear without great harm to himself.

"Ah! sir," said Sir Bagdemagus, "I shall
to-morrow try this adventure, and if I do not
succeed you shall take it upon you, for I am
sure you shall not fail."

"Sir," said Galahad, "I agree with this,
for I have no shield. On the morrow Sir
Bagdemagus asked where the shield was.
Straightway a monk led him behind an altar,
where the shield hung as white as any snow,
but in the middle of it was a red cross.

"Sirs," said the monk, "this shield can only
be borne by the one who is the worthiest
knight in the world, therefore I advise you
to think over what you are doing."

"Well," replied Bagdemagus, "I am sure
I am not the best knight in the world, but I
shall try to bear it. So, asking Sir Galahad
to stay there till he saw how he fared, he
took the red-cross shield out of the abbey.

He took with him a good squire, who was to bring tidings back to Sir Galahad as to how he fared, and rode away.

When they had ridden for two miles they came to a fair valley in front of a hermitage, from which came forth a knight clad in white armour, horse and all. He came as fast as his horse could run, with his spear in rest.

Sir Bagdemagus attacked him, and broke his spear upon the White Knight. But the other struck him so hard that he broke through his armour and wounded him on the right shoulder, for at that time the shield did not cover him, and so Bagdemagus was unhorsed.

Thereupon the White Knight alighted from his horse and took the white shield from Sir Bagdemagus, saying: " Knight, you have done foolishly, for this shield ought not to be borne except by one who has no equal living."

Then he came to the squire and said: " Bear this shield unto the good knight Sir Galahad, whom you left in the abbey, and greet him well from me." The squire wished to know his name, but the knight said it was not for him or any other earthly man to know it. But before going, the squire went unto Bagdemagus and asked whether he was sore wounded or not.

"Yea, forsooth," said he, "I shall escape with difficulty from death." Then the squire brought his horse, and carried him with great pain unto the abbey. He was taken down softly from the horse, his armour taken off, and he was laid in a bed. There his wounds were carefully attended to, and as the book telleth, he lay there for a long time, and escaped barely with his life.

"Sir," said the squire when he returned to Sir Galahad, "the knight that wounded Bagdemagus sends you greeting, and bids you bear this shield through all the adventures that will befall you."

Then Sir Galahad asked for his arms, mounted his horse, and, commending himself to God, hung the white shield about his neck. Sir Uwaine wished to go with him, but Sir Galahad said he would go alone save the squire.

So he departed, and in a short time came to the hermitage where the White Knight waited for him. They saluted each other courteously, and the knight told him of the many marvels of the shield.

"Sir," said the knight, "it happened thirty-two years after the passion of our Lord Jesus

Christ that Joseph of Arimathea, the gentle knight, who took down our Lord from off the Cross, departed from Jerusalem with a great number of his kindred with him. He passed on till they came to a city called Sarras.

"At the same time that Joseph came to Sarras, there was a king in that city called Evelake, who had waged war against the Saracens. There Joseph made this shield for him, in the name of Him that died upon the Cross. By this means he had victory over his enemies.

"For when King Evelake was in the battle, there was a cloth set before the shield, and when he was in greatest danger the cloth was taken away. Then his enemies saw the figure of a man on the Cross. This sight caused them to flee.

"Soon afterwards another great marvel happened: the cross of the shield disappeared, and no man could say how it took place. As the result of all this King Evelake was baptized, and for the most part all the people of Sarras.

"Soon Joseph departed from the city of Sarras, and King Evelake would go with him whether he would or not, and they came unto this land of Britain. There he was thrown into prison. But news of his imprisonment came to a worthy man named Mondrames, who, when he heard it, at once gathered all his people together and set out for Great Britain to set Joseph free. This he was able to accomplish, and as a result all the people of Britain were turned to the Christian faith.

"Not long after, when Joseph of Arimathea lay on his deathbed, King Evelake came to his bedside, and with great sorrow asked that Joseph should give him some token that would lead him to think of him, for love of whom he had left his own country. So Joseph called for the shield which had been made at Sarras, and with his own blood he put upon it a cross.

"King Evelake would by this token always remember the old knight's love, for he would never be able to look upon the shield without thinking of him. He also told him that the cross would always be as fresh as it was then. No man would ever bear the shield about his neck without being sorry for doing so, until the good knight Galahad, the last of Joseph's lineage, would bear it, and do marvellous deeds while bearing it.

"He instructed King Evelake to place it in the hermitage of Nacien, for Galahad would

come for it on the fifteenth day after he had
received the order of knighthood. To-day is
the time set that you shall have King Evelake's shield."

Then having said this, the White Knight
vanished away, and Sir Galahad rode back with
his squire to the abbey.

CHAPTER IX

THE KNIGHT OF THE ILL-SHAPEN COAT

Upon a day of spring, when the skies were
bright and the earth was fair with promise,
there came to the Court of King Arthur a
young man of whom no knight present knew
anything, and, paying his respects to the King,
he asked to be made one of his knights.

King Arthur looked upon the youth, and he
was well pleased with him. He had a fine
form and held himself nobly. Upon his back
he had a coat made of cloth of gold, but which
fitted him so ill, that it did not matter much
what kind of form he had beneath.

The King said: "Tell me, brave youth,
what is your name?"

The youth replied: "Sir, my name is Brew-nor-le-Noir. If you will make me a knight, you will find out about my high birth."

Then said Sir Kay, who was the Steward: "Let your name be what it may, the name you merit is The Ill-shapen Coat; for never have I seen a less well-shapen coat."

Now King Arthur was ever a gentle knight, and he did not like this comely boy to be vexed. So he asked him: "Tell me the meaning of the coat, for I am sure it is not worn without a cause."

The youth replied: "Sir, I had a father, a good and gentle knight. One day it happened that he fell asleep, wearing this coat. While he slept, one whose name I do not know fell upon him, and hacked him to pieces —a wicked deed! Wherefore as the coat was then, so I now wear it; and I shall wear it upon me till I have met the slayer of my father."

When this story was told, two of King Arthur's knights pleaded that the boy should be made a knight. "For he has a noble form," said they, "and an eye that falls not. We say that there lies in him the making of a right noble knight."

So the King agreed, saying that on the morrow he would grant their prayer.

Now on the morrow the King went out to hunt, taking a great number of his knights with him. With those that stayed behind he left the stranger, whom Sir Kay had named The Ill-shapen Coat. They were, all of them, with Queen Guinevere.

As the knights waited on her in the King's absence, there broke loose from its tower of stone a great lion that was caged there, and came after the Queen and her knights with great fury.

Then the knights all fled but twelve of them. These twelve did not know how to serve the Queen and themselves.

But the stranger drew out his sword, and without more ado he set himself upon the lion, and gave it such a blow on the head that it fell dead.

Then he took his place, but did not say a word.

Now when King Arthur came back from the chase, he was told what the stranger had done when he was away with the older knights, how with his own hand he had slain the lion, and how no knight had thought to do this thing.

The King said: "It was a true word which he spoke to me that I would soon find out his high birth. This lad will prove a brave knight." And with that, he made him a knight.

Then the youth asked leave of the King to be called the Knight of the Ill-shapen Coat. This request the King granted, though he was ill pleased that the knight had been so named.

Later, but on the same day, there came to King Arthur's Court a damsel with eyes of fire, and a mouth of sweetness, who carried with her a great black shield. Upon this shield was a white hand that held a sword.

When King Arthur saw her, he asked her what her errand was, and she replied:

"Sir, I have travelled many nights and days to bring this shield to your Court. For it belonged to a knight who had vowed to do some great deed of arms. But he had an adventure in which he was so badly wounded that he died. He was a knight of great purity and courage. I seek one like unto him that he may take upon himself the quest of the shield. But I am sure that it is a hard quest."

Now no knight said he would take the quest upon himself.

Then Sir Kay came forward and took the shield in his hand and held it.

The damsel asked him what his name was; and when she had heard it, she said: "The quest is not yours, for it requires a better knight than you, Sir Kay."

On hearing this, Sir Kay replied with anger: " I only took the shield to feel the weight of it, for I do not like either you or your quest."

But the damsel did not heed him or his wrath, and having looked long at the knights, she said she did not like any of them.

Then came forward the Knight of the Ill-shapen Coat, saying that he would take upon himself the quest with great joy, since he had but that day been made a knight and was eager for adventure.

"What is your name?" asked the damsel, fixing her glance upon him.

He replied: "My name is The Ill-shapen Coat."

" 'Tis a fit name," said she, "for never have I seen such a coat. As for the adventure, it is likely that it will bruise your skin to match your coat, if you take it upon you."

"Nevertheless," said the knight, " I will take it, and whithersoever it leads me, thither

I will go. Wherefore I pray you that we start at once."

Soon she prepared to depart. There was brought to the knight a great horse, and his armour, and his spear. When he was ready, he bade them farewell for a time. And with the maiden he set forth upon the quest.

Riding beside him, she shed upon him the fire of her eyes. And from the sweetness of her mouth she sent out words that were not sweet, but sour. The knight thought that she scorned him for his youth's sake and because he had never gone on a quest before.

Now they had gone but a little way when Sir Dagonet came riding behind them. It was he who was the King's fool. When he had overtaken the Knight of the Ill-shapen Coat, he called to him that he would joust with him.

Then Sir Knight of the Ill-shapen Coat smote his horse, and he left them.

Ever as they rode on, the maiden made greater mock of the knight, telling him that the King had sent a fool after him to joust with him, since he thought him worthy of no other knight. But the knight did not reply to her words.

Then they rode on, and when they had gone

two days' journey they came upon Sir Bleoberis, who offered to joust with Sir Knight of the Ill-shapen Coat.

When he had agreed to this, Sir Bleoberis showered on him such blows that he speedily unhorsed him and laid him on the ground.

"By my word," cried the Knight of the Ill-shapen Coat, "you shall finish the fight on foot!" And he made himself ready in a fury.

"Nay," said Sir Bleoberis, "I am not minded to fight on foot, I did not offer to do so." And with that he rode away.

Then did the damsel cast the fire of her eyes anew upon the Knight of the Ill-shapen Coat, and twisting the sweetness of her mouth, she said: "You have failed in a new thing, coward knight!"

"Misname me not!" cried he. "Surely it is not a cowardly thing to be unhorsed by such a knight as Sir Bleoberis. In a short time I shall prove to you that I am no coward."

But the damsel would not be quieted. And she kept on speaking bitter words to him. Thus they went on, having no great pleasure in each other's company.

When they had gone another two days'

journey, they met Sir Palomides, a brave knight, who offered to the Knight of the Ill-shapen Coat that he would joust with him.

"Now we shall see the same thing as before!" cried the damsel in the knight's ear. And indeed so it proved, for Sir Palomides gave the younger knight so hard a blow that he sent him headlong to the ground.

Then was the Knight of the Ill-shapen Coat again angry, the more so as he expected the damsel to make a fool of him. He would have fought with Sir Palomides on foot, but the knight would not do so. Therefore they parted.

The damsel's speech was even more bitter against the young knight.

Now they had gone on but a little way when they came upon Sir Modred, who had been but a little way in front of them, and he journeyed with them.

"Now," thought the Knight of the Ill-shapen Coat, "she will cease to speak bitterly to me, being ashamed to do so when another knight is with me."

But not so; the maiden did not pay any heed to Sir Modred, and, if possible, her speech was

less sweet than before. At this Sir Modred
wondered much.

The three had journeyed another three days
when they came to a castle. Now in passing
this castle a knight had either to joust or be
taken prisoner. For such was the custom.

Then Sir Modred and the Knight of the
Ill-shapen Coat made ready, and when they
were in front of the castle there came out two
knights, who rode with great skill.

"Now we shall see again that which we
have seen," said the damsel.

But the younger knight took no heed of her,
and as for Sir Modred, he did not know what
she meant.

Then came the knights of the castle against
them. One of them rushed at Sir Modred and
laid him on the ground. The other flew upon
the younger knight, and they fought with such
fury that they came both to the ground.

Now the Knight of the Ill-shapen Coat
sprang upon his enemy's horse, and rushing
upon that knight who had unhorsed Sir Modred, he wounded him so that he fought no
more.

Then he came back to his own man—who
had mounted the horse of the young knight—

and fell upon him. Having unhorsed him, he killed him. But the other knight had taken flight into the castle before he met his death, and the Knight of the Ill-shapen Coat after him. When he was dead, there came nearly one hundred knights and attacked the Knight of the Ill-shapen Coat.

He set his back against the wall of a lady's room and fought with them.

Then came a lady and took the horse of the young knight, which he had left behind him. She led it away while he fought with the hundred knights, and tied it to the gate.

Then she came near to him and whispered: "Knight, you do well, but how will you gain your horse and escape, for I have tied it to yonder gate; and all these knights lie in the way."

When the Knight of the Ill-shapen Coat heard this whisper of the lady, he set his shield to cover him, and threw himself upon the knights where they were thickest, and made his way through them. When he reached the gate, he saw four knights there, and two of these he slew, and the other two he attacked so strongly that they fled. Then he mounted his horse and rode away.

Having come upon the maiden and Sir Modred, where they stood talking about him, for the damsel was sure that he was slain, he told them how he had won his way out, in spite of the hundred knights and the trick of the lady.

But the damsel did not believe him. And she called to her a squire in whom she had great trust, who went with her on all her journeys. And before the two knights, she bade him ride to the castle and ask how the knight fared who had fought them.

Now the squire was not a long time away, and when he came back he spake out what the knights had told him. They said they had never seen a knight such as that knight about whom he asked, and how he had slain twelve of them, and had won his way to the gate, and had ridden away.

Then looked Sir Modred sideways at the maiden; but the younger knight turned away his head. As for that ill-spoken damsel, she hung her head and said not one word.

Now they rode on; and as they rode, the young knight being silent, and wrapt in his thoughts, Sir Modred thought well to speak to the maiden about the wrong she did her knight. And, regarding the matter of Sir

Bleoberis and Sir Palomides, he reminded her how easy it was for an elder knight to unseat one younger, who was yet unused to his steed.

Of the refusal of the knights to fight with the younger knight on foot, he told her that it might well be that they so refused lest they should be overcome by the young knight, who doubtless was better able to show his valour when his horse no longer hampered him.

To these words the damsel listened, making no reply. But when the day was over, she was as bitter to the young knight as before.

CHAPTER X

FURTHER ADVENTURES OF THE KNIGHT OF THE ILL-SHAPEN COAT

FOR seven days they journeyed. At the end of that time there overtook them that knight, most renowned of all King Arthur's Round Table, Sir Launcelot of the Lake.

Then went away Sir Modred, going his own way, and Sir Launcelot became their companion instead, but they did not know who he was.

The Knight of the Ill-shapen Coat thought,

"Will she speak bitterly to me again before this stranger?"

And indeed, the damsel began at once to do so, twitting him on the unlucky events that had happened on their journey. Such things as had happened to do the young knight honour, she either made no mention of or twisted them to suit herself.

Then was Sir Launcelot angry, for he did not like to hear the damsel speak in this way, and he found fault with her sharply for behaving so unkindly to her knight.

Not a whit cared she. True, she let the younger knight rest in peace for a time. But that was because she now began to speak as bitter words to Sir Launcelot. And, knowing him not, she was as unkind to him as she had been to her knight.

When they had gone some distance in this way, Sir Launcelot left them for a time, to go upon a quest of his own.

Then came the Knight of the Ill-shapen Coat and his damsel to the castle Pendragon. From the castle there came riding out six knights, and one of them offered to joust with him.

Thereupon the Knight of the Ill-shapen

Coat smote him. He had no sooner done so than the other five knights fell upon him in a body and all unawares, in a most unknightly way. They smote him from his horse, and took him prisoner into the castle, and the unkind damsel with him.

After a little while came Sir Launcelot riding that way, for he had finished his quest, and would now like to find the Knight of the Ill-shapen Coat. On the way, before he had come to the castle Pendragon, he came upon a knight, who offered to joust with him. So they fell to.

Then Sir Launcelot smote the knight from his horse, and they fought on foot, and that right mightily, till at last Sir Launcelot brought the knight to his knees.

Then the knight gave himself up, and he asked Sir Launcelot to tell him his name, for he had never before been brought to yield, nor had he gone through such a fight as this with Sir Launcelot.

Sir Launcelot told him that he was Sir Launcelot of the Lake. And the knight related to him how a knight had been taken prisoner at the castle Pendragon and a damsel with him.

"I am very sure that he is my comrade," said Sir Launcelot, "and I must go and rescue him." With that he departed. The knight could hardly believe that he had fought with the great Sir Launcelot, and he thought it small shame to be defeated by such a noble knight.

When Sir Launcelot reached the castle Pendragon there came out six knights to meet him. They fell upon him, all at one time, and with great fury. Then Sir Launcelot drove his spear with such skill that he sorely wounded three of them, and left them upon the ground.

As he went on he met the other three, who had drawn aside the better to fall on him anew, and he wounded them also. After that, he rode with great fury into the castle. Then came the lord of the castle to do battle with Sir Launcelot. They flew together with a great noise, and with such force that their horses fell to the ground.

Therefore they betook themselves to their swords, and fought on foot, and their strokes fell so swiftly that they could not be counted.

Then Sir Launcelot gave a blow so great that he brought the lord of the castle to his knees, and he pulled his helmet from him.

Therefore the lord, seeing that he would be slain, gave himself up to Sir Launcelot, and Sir Launcelot bade him set free all the prisoners that he held within the castle.

When this was done, there was found among them the Knight of the Ill-shapen Coat and his damsel. When they found themselves set free, the knight sought his horse and armour that he might go on his way.

Then came into the castle a squire from that knight with whom Sir Launcelot had jousted on his way to the castle Pendragon. He wished to know how Sir Launcelot had fared. But Sir Launcelot had already ridden from the castle.

Then was the lord of the castle very glad that he had been overcome by a knight of such great fame as Sir Launcelot. And the Knight of the Ill-shapen Coat knew who it was who had ridden with them, and he was right joyful. But the damsel was heavy with shame and said not one word.

Now when the damsel and her knight had left that castle named Pendragon, and had journeyed on, they came upon Sir Launcelot, who was ahead, and overtook him.

Then they thanked him for the many mighty

deeds he had done for them, and they begged that he would still be their companion.

"For a while yet will I ride with you," said Sir Launcelot, "but on this condition let it be, that the damsel shall no more speak bitter words to her knight. For I think that he is a right noble knight, and it is for his sake and to save him from death that I go with you now."

"Alack," cried the damsel, "think not that I am found fault with because in my heart I thought ill of the knight! Nay, rather was my heart filled with love. For that reason I spoke bitterly to him, for I knew the quest to be one full of danger. I wished to drive him away by my bitter words."

And from that moment she did not say another bitter word to her knight.

Now they had done some days' journey when they came upon the borders of a new country, and they found there a village, with a strong bridge like a fortress. And upon the bridge were gathered a number of knights, who stopped the way.

When they beheld Sir Launcelot and the Knight of the Ill-shapen Coat, they called to them how, because of the black shield which one of them carried, they might not enter within the bridge, except one at a time.

Then said the younger knight to Sir Launcelot: "I pray you, let me enter first, for I wish to take upon me this adventure. If I fare well in it, then I will send for you. And if I die, I die as a knight should."

Now Sir Launcelot was unwilling to allow him to go; but after a time he granted his request.

Then the Knight of the Ill-shapen Coat entered within the bridge. There he met two brothers, and they did battle with him. Now the knight smote first the one and afterwards the other from his horse. Then did they take their swords and rush upon him, and he, having got down also from his horse, met them; and they showered on him heavy blows with great fury. They wounded him on the head and shoulders, and on his breast.

"The pain of my wounds is bitter, but the pain of defeat is worse," thought the young knight, and he drew together what strength was left him. Falling upon them anew, with a mighty courage, he brought both knights to their knees, so that they had to yield themselves to him or be slain.

So they gave themselves up to him. And the young knight chose that horse which was best, and rode on. Having reached another bridge and fortress, he met another brother, whose name was Sir Plenorius. With him he fought till their horses fell.

Upon this they went on with the fight on foot and with their swords. And for two long hours they fought, and longer, and gave mighty strokes.

Sir Launcelot, as he stood watching, was filled with fear for the young knight, for he had already fought one battle with great skill, receiving many wounds. At last he fell to the ground through weakness and the pain of his wounds.

But Sir Plenorius had pity on him, saying: "Had you been as fresh as I was when I met you, this thing had not come about. You have fought right well, and I will tend you with all gentleness till your hurt is cured." So he carried him into the tower.

Then came a voice calling to Sir Plenorius, bidding him that he should give up his prisoner or else do battle with the knight who called him.

And Sir Plenorius mounted his horse and

rode to the spot where Sir Launcelot stood calling. Like two mighty rushing winds the two knights flew together.

Then they struck at one another great blows with their spears, till their horses fell with the fury of them.

When the horses had fallen, they left them there, and fell upon each other with their swords. They fought with a fury so great that no man has ever seen the like.

As for the damsel, she saw that Sir Launcelot thought her knight of right good account thus to fight for him.

And after a time Sir Launcelot brought Sir Plenorius to his knees, but that only after many hard blows, for he was a brave knight and well skilled.

When Sir Plenorius had yielded himself, Sir Launcelot met three others of his brethren, and defeated these also. When he had done this, he would have given to the Knight of the Ill-shapen Coat the fortresses and the bridges.

But the knight would not take any of them. "Nay," said he, "I will not take these from Sir Plenorius, for he is a right brave knight and of a kind heart. My lord, I pray you instead to let them remain with Sir Plenorius and his brethren, on this condition: that he come to King Arthur's Court and be a knight of his, and his brethren with him."

Now Sir Launcelot agreed to this, for he had a liking for Sir Plenorius, believing him to be a brave knight and of a pure life.

Sir Launcelot remained in that country till the young knight was cured of his wounds He fared well, having plenty of pleasure and many good games.

When the days of the knight's sickness were passed, they returned to the Court of King Arthur, the quest of the black shield having been finished. As they passed the castle of Pendragon, Sir Launcelot gave that castle to the Knight of the Ill-shapen Coat, since the lord of it would not become King Arthur's knight.

At Pentecost following, the Knight of the Ill-shapen Coat was made a knight of the King's Round Table, and he proved a mighty knight and noble.

For his wife he chose that damsel who had brought to him the black shield. And she twisted no more the sweetness of her lips, but gave him kindly words.

CHAPTER XI

THE KNIGHT OF THE KITCHEN

KING ARTHUR had gone with his knights of the Round Table to Kin-Kenadon, which is upon the sand near Wales, there to keep the great feast of Pentecost. And, as was his custom, he would taste no food till he had heard of some adventure.

Then Sir Gawaine, his nephew, looked out of the castle window, and he saw three men on horseback, who came rapidly toward the castle. Behind them was a dwarf, who ran on foot.

Sir Gawaine then said to the King: "My lord, wait no longer for your dinner, for here comes an adventure toward you, hard and fast."

King Arthur now went to the hall, where dinner was laid, and with him other kings that were his guests, and all his knights.

They had just taken their seats when these three men, whom Sir Gawaine had seen, entered the hall.

Now two of them were very tall, but the third was taller still. As he came he leaned on the shoulders of the other two men—for he walked between them—as if he could not walk alone.

Yet he was strong of body, and of a healthy colour, and he was not wounded.

When he had come to the place where King Arthur sat, the young man raised himself with ease, as if he had had no reason for leaning on the men.

Then he spoke to the King, saying: "Sir, here I have come to ask you to grant me three gifts. But of these I will ask but one at this time, and the other two on Pentecost a year hence."

Now King Arthur, looking upon the young man, found him straight and fair, and manly. And, although he knew nothing of him, he liked him well. He said: "Ask, my son, and your request will be granted you."

"Sir," said the stranger, "the gift I ask of you is this, that for twelve months you will provide me with meat and drink."

"Nay," said the King, "call not this a gift. Is it not the due of any man who ha~ need of it? Eat and drink what you will, but ask of me that which shall be more worthy of you, for I believe you are of noble blood."

"Of that I can tell you nothing," said the young man; "neither do I ask anything but that you provide me with meat and drink till these twelve months are past."

Then the King called Sir Kay, who was Steward, and bade him that he should give the young man such food and drink as he needed day by day, for one year.

And the King, who was ever generous, told Sir Kay to provide the young man with gentle food. "For," said he, "I am sure he is of gentle blood."

But Sir Kay was very angry, for he did not like the stranger, and did not care for the task the King had given him. "This fellow has no gentle blood," said he, "or he would have asked for a horse and armour, as becomes a knight, that he might do noble deeds. Nay, he is some low fellow, who would sup from a full dish. For as his request is, so is he. To-day I give him the name that will serve him well. He shall be called Beaumains, that is to say, Fair Hands, for his hands are large and fair; and I feel certain he uses them well when he sups from the King's bowl."

At this speech two knights were very angry,

and these were that brave knight Sir Launcelot, and Sir Gawaine, who was son to the King's sister. They told Sir Kay to stop his mocking, which they were sure he would be sorry for, since they believed the stranger would prove one day to be a most noble knight.

"Nay," said Sir Kay, "he shall be a kitchen knight, for there is his place. I shall feed him in the kitchen till he is as broad as he is long."

With that Sir Kay made his way to his own place at table and seated himself.

And the two men who had come with the young man having left him, the stranger went to the hall door, and sat among the boys and serving-men and shared their food.

At night he slept with the youths of the kitchen, for this was Sir Kay's orders. And in the daytime he supped with them again.

Then were Sir Launcelot and Sir Gawaine again angry. But Sir Kay took no heed of their words. And they would have had it that Beaumains should have meat and drink and lodging from them, but the young man would not take them.

In all things he desired to have himself treated as Sir Kay ordered, and with meekness he bore that knight's unkind words. Yet was the young man of a high spirit and great courage. Nor was he without skill in the throwing of bar or stone, for no one could throw as far as he.

And where there was jousting of knights or other brave play, there Beaumains was to be found, taking great delight in these things.

Now twelve months had passed, and King Arthur kept again the great feast of Pentecost. And, as before, he would not sit down to meat till news of some adventure was brought to him.

And as he waited there came into the hall a damsel. She was proud-looking, but she had a smile that was wonderfully sweet, though in truth she could be moved to smile very seldom. She saluted the King, and asked him for a knight who would help a lady in trouble.

"Who is this lady?" asked the King. "And from what distress does she suffer?"

"Nay," said the damsel, "I am not allowed to tell you her name; but she is of right noble blood, and has wide lands of her own. And her trouble is that she is besieged by a knight, so that she may not leave her own castle. And the knight is that knight who is known as the Knight of the Reed Lands."

"I know nothing of him," said King Arthur.

But Sir Gawaine said: "I know more of him than I well care to know. For I once escaped from this knight, and that with great difficulty. He has, it is said, the strength of seven men."

Then the King said: "Fair maid, I do not doubt but that many a knight here present would gladly ride to the help of your lady; but because you will state neither her name nor where she stays, I am unwilling to let any knight go."

"Then I must go somewhere else," said the damsel.

But at that moment Beaumains came forward from the kitchen, and, saluting the King, he said: "Sir, the time is now come when I would ask of you those other two gifts of which I told you. The first gift I ask is that you will permit me to go with the damsel and take this adventure upon me; and the second is that Sir Launcelot may ride after me to make me a knight when the time arrives. For I would like to be made a knight by him."

Then said the King: "My son, I grant you what you ask."

When she heard this, the damsel was not well

pleased, and she cried at the King because he refused her a knight for her quest, and had given her a kitchen knight; and she was very angry.

But Beaumains did not at all heed her anger. And someone came to him to tell him that a dwarf had arrived bringing him his horse and armour. Therefore he went away to make himself ready for the adventure.

And when he was made ready, there were none that did not wonder at the richness of his armour; but he was without spear or shield.

When Beaumains had ridden away with the damsel, and with the dwarf following after, Sir Kay said: "I will go after this kitchen boy of mine, and see if the fellow knows his master."

"Nay," said Sir Launcelot and Sir Gawaine, "leave the youth in peace. You have already insulted him very badly, and have laid up for yourself future shame."

But Sir Kay did not heed them, and, getting upon his horse, he rode after Beaumains.

And when he was yet some distance behind him, he cried out to the youth to wait for him. "It is I. Do you not know me, Beaumains?" he cried.

Then Beaumains drew in his horse and

waited, and the damsel looked upon the youth with scorn.

When Sir Kay came near, Beaumains cried boldly: "Indeed I know you well, for you are a knight who has shown me little kindness and has ever used me badly."

At these words Sir Kay flew into a fury, and rushed at him with his spear. But Beaumains, having no spear, gripped his sword and turned the blow aside, and then another blow. Then Beaumains leant forward, and thrust the knight through with his sword. It was a neat thrust that he gave, and Sir Kay fell to the ground with a great wound.

Beaumains now took the spear and shield of Sir Kay, and had them for his own. He bade the dwarf mount Sir Kay's horse and go no more on foot. He had just done this, when he saw Sir Launcelot, who was following him.

Then he offered Sir Launcelot to joust with him, and immediately they rushed at one another, while the damsel looked on with her proud head high in the air.

"I wonder at you, Sir Launcelot, that you should joust with a kitchen knave!" she cried, mocking.

But neither Sir Launcelot nor Beaumains

gave heed to her, for they were thinking of a different matter.

The kitchen boy dealt great blows, and Sir Launcelot had much ado to hold himself against them, for they were more like the blows of a giant than a man.

At last they both came to the ground because of the force of their blows, and Sir Launcelot helped Beaumains to get clear of his horse. Then they fell upon each other with their swords.

After they had fought till they were weary— and Sir Launcelot was almost overcome with the difficulty of defending himself from Beaumains, for the kitchen boy fought as bravely on foot as on his horse—Sir Launcelot cried: "Hold, Beaumains! have we not fought enough to show your skill? Our quarrel is not so great that we need to fight further."

Beaumains at once replied, dropping his hand: "I have no quarrel with you, Sir Launcelot, and I give you thanks that you did not refuse to joust with me. I would like to be knighted by you before I go farther on my adventure. Do you think that I may prove a true knight?"

"Indeed I have little doubt of it!" said Sir Launcelot, "for I had greater difficulty with you than I have had in jousting with any champion."

With that he made Beaumains a knight with right good will; afterwards setting himself to see to Sir Kay and his hurt.

Sir Beaumains and the damsel rode on, and immediately she began to chide him, calling him the kitchen knight, and by other means making little of him.

Ever she wondered that Sir Launcelot should have thought him worthy to joust with, and ever she mourned that Sir Kay should have been wounded by so sorry a knight.

But Sir Beaumains would not leave her, in spite of her unkind words, for he had made up his mind to go upon this adventure.

As they pressed on through the woods, there came running towards them, as fast as he could, a fellow whose clothes were very badly torn, as if others had fought with him, and he looked very much afraid.

Then Sir Beaumains called to him, asking what was wrong with him. He replied that his lord had been set upon in the wood by six thieves, and that he himself was fleeing from these robbers, who had ill-used him. They had bound his lord so that he could not flee.

Sir Beaumains had no sooner heard this story than he bade the fellow guide him to the spot where his master lay. Having reached it, he fell furiously upon the thieves, slaying three of them, and putting the other three to flight. Then he followed these three and slew them also, lest they should do mischief to other good knights.

Having finished this adventure with success, he went with the rescued knight to his castle, which was at no great distance. There he and the damsel passed the night, and next morning went once again on their way.

Now they came to a great forest, and when they had gone through part of it, they found a river, which had but one crossing. And this crossing two knights held, waiting on the other side.

"Come, will you fight with those bold knights, kitchen knave?" asked the damsel, "or shall we return, and go by another way?"

"I will not return," said Sir Beaumains; "and I do not think well of you that you should ask me to do so."

Then, without further waste of words, he rode into the stream, and immediately one of the knights advanced to meet him.

Halfway across the stream they met, and there they fought bravely. But Sir Beaumains gave the strange knight a blow on the head that was too strong for him, and he was overcome and fell into the stream.

Then Sir Beaumains rode forward to meet that other knight, and having met him, he slew him also. And when he had done this, he brought the damsel across the stream.

But she gave him no thanks for what he had done. "Keep at a distance, kitchen knight," cried she, "for I do not like the air of the kitchen which hangs about you! Do not think that I esteem you more highly on account of your deeds. For I know well that the first knight fell into the stream and was drowned because his foot caught upon a stone. As for the second, you crept up behind him or you would not have slain him. Away from me! I do not like you by my side."

But Sir Beaumains did not move from her side one inch. As for her bitter words, he rode on with an air as if he had not heard them For this reason she liked him the less.

CHAPTER XII

SIR BEAUMAINS MEETS SEVERAL KNIGHTS

AFTER a time Sir Beaumains and the damsel came to a black country, and in the black country grew a black hawthorn, and on the black hawthorn hung a black shield, and by the shield was a black spear, and by the spear a great black horse, and a black stone was near the horse.

"Now are we in the lands of the Black Knight," said the damsel. "Fly, kitchen knight, while there is time, before he catches sight of you!"

"Nay, I like better to ride forward," said Sir Beaumains; "for I have a great wish to see this Black Knight." But he did not look at the damsel.

Then came the Black Knight riding toward them on a horse even blacker than the first they had seen, and clad in black armour. His eyes were as black as coals. Immediately the damsel began to make moan to him, as if in pity, that he would spare Sir Beaumains.

"For this is but a kitchen knave," said she, "whose head has been turned through riding with a lady of my rank. I pray you, Sir Knight, to do him no harm."

The Black Knight said: "He is not dressed as a kitchen knave, but as a knight."

"So he thinks himself," said the damsel; "nevertheless he is but a kitchen knave, as I have said. Many knightly deeds has he done, but not by skill. And he has killed good knights."

"Damsel," said the Black Knight, "I shall do him no harm. Bid him only that he leave with me his horse and armour, for I would have him do no more evil."

Then cried Sir Beaumains in a high voice: "Sir, you talk lightly of my horse and armour; but know that they are mine, not yours, and that I will not give them up. Yet will I pass through your lands, and from them, and go upon my way."

At these words the Black Knight became wrathful, and he warned Sir Beaumains that he would fight with him. So they drew apart some distance, and then rushed together. With the force of the blow he gave against the shield of Beaumains, the spear of the Black Knight broke. At the same moment Sir Beaumains thrust his spear into the Black

Knight's side, so that it broke also, leaving the point still in his body.

Yet the Black Knight drew his sword, and fought with that, and he gave Sir Beaumains many sore strokes before he died from his wound.

Sir Beaumains, seeing him to be so well armed and mounted, lighted down and took his horse and armour. Then he rode after the damsel, who had gone on ahead.

"Behold him! how pleased he is with himself!" cried she. "So you have slain the Black Knight, kitchen knave. But before long you shall meet his two brethren, and they will make you pay dearly for it. Yet I would like to be rid of you before then. I do not wish to see you beaten, kitchen knave."

"Damsel," said Sir Beaumains, "whether I am a kitchen knave or not, is not known to you. But this you may know, that I will not leave you till this quest is done."

"Upon your own head be it!" said the damsel; and Sir Beaumains thought she sighed. Then they rode on in silence.

When they had gone some days' journey, they came upon a knight clad all in green, who rode toward them, and stood in the way before them.

And he called to the damsel: "Is it my brother the Black Knight that you have brought with you?"

"Nay," cried she, "it is not your brother the Black Knight, but a boy from King Arthur's kitchen, who has slain him through some evil chance, and stolen his horse and armour."

"Alas! that such a good knight should be overthrown by a poor knave," cried the knight in green. "But for this you shall die at once."

"I defy you!" said Sir Beaumains; "and know that I fought your brother knightly."

When the Green Knight heard these words, he plucked from under a thorn a green horn that hung there, and blew on it three notes. And immediately there appeared three fair maidens clad in green. They dressed him in green armour, and brought him a green horse, and a spear that was green.

"Now, fellow," cried the Green Knight, "I am ready to do battle with you."

And he rushed upon Sir Beaumains.

They thrust at each other with their spears, mighty and fierce blows. And after they had come down off their horses, they fought furiously with their swords. The fight lasted for a long time.

"For shame, Green Knight!" cried the damsel, "that you fight so long with a kitchen knave, who has the smell of meats yet upon him."

When the Green Knight heard this speech he was angry, and ran at Sir Beaumains again. With a fierce thrust he struck at him, and broke his shield in two.

But Sir Beaumains repaid the blow with one as fierce, and followed it with a buffet on the helmet which sent the Green Knight to his knees. Then the Green Knight prayed for mercy, for he saw by the fury of Sir Beaumains that he was near his death.

"Nay," said Sir Beaumains, "you may withhold your prayer, Green Knight, for there is nothing that will make me have mercy upon you, save only if this damsel ask me for your life."

The damsel at once said: "I will never ask you, kitchen knight!"

"Then the Green Knight shall die!" said Sir Beaumains.

The Green Knight prayed again for his life, saying: "My life shall be at your service, Sir Knight, and the lives of the thirty knights whom I command."

"Your words avail you nothing," said Sir Beaumains. "I will spare you only if this maid asks it."

Then the Green Knight begged the damsel that she should ask for his life.

"Shall I ask this from a kitchen knave?" she asked, with a high chin.

"Nay," said the Green Knight, "I am sure this is no kitchen knight, but a right noble knight."

Yet the damsel stood pouting.

Then Sir Beaumains began to unlace the helmet of the Green Knight as if to slay him.

"Hold!" cried the maid. "If you will have it so, you will have it so, and I am unwilling that the Green Knight should perish. I pray you spare him!"

"I grant you your life," said Sir Beaumains; and he spared the Green Knight's life because of the damsel's asking.

That night they stayed at the Green Knight's castle, which was near; and on the morrow they went their way.

Then when they had left the lands of the Green Knight, the damsel again began to speak with scorn to Sir Beaumains. "What! are you still with me, kitchen knave?" said she. "Do not think that I esteem you better for this adventure with the Green Knight. For you shall, before this quest is ended, meet one worse than he. I advise you to say farewell and go."

Sir Beaumains replied: "Cease your idle words! Have you not learned that I will not leave you till this quest is ended?"

They now rode on for two days, when they came to a fair plain by the sea, where they saw the walls and towers of a castle, and a fair meadow about it. And the lord of the tower looked out of a window and saw them approach.

Then he left the tower, and came to meet them. And when he had come pretty near, he cried to Sir Beaumains: "Brother, is it you? Where are you going?"

But the damsel cried: "This is not your brother, the Black Knight, but a kitchen knave who has by an evil chance slain him."

Now the lord of the tower was clad in red, and he was mounted upon a horse that was of a ruddy colour, and he had a red spear. When he had got ready, he fought with Sir Beaumains, first with his spear, and afterwards on foot and with his sword.

To him it happened as had befallen the Green Knight, his brother, for he was overthrown, and Sir Beaumains saved his life only on the asking of the damsel.

Then the Red Knight promised his service, and the service of fifty knights, when Sir Beaumains should call upon them.

And Sir Beaumains and his damsel abode with him that night at his castle, and afterwards went upon their way.

Again the damsel mocked Sir Beaumains, and would have driven him from her side.

Then came they to the lands of Sir Persaunt of Ind, and with him also Sir Beaumains did battle, and had victory. And Sir Persaunt promised the service of one hundred knights.

And having passed the night at his castle, they went on. But the damsel chided no more, for she began to see how brave a knight was this Sir Beaumains, and she thought he was, in spite of all, of noble blood.

Thus she remained silent, ashamed of her former speeches. And in this wise they drew near to the castle of the lady, Dame Lyonesse, round which a siege was laid.

"Now are we come to the dangerous adventure," said the damsel, "for yonder is the castle of the Lady Lyonesse, who is my sister. And the knight who thus besieges her, is he not the Red Knight of the Reed Lands, than whom there is none greater? Alas! Sir Knight, I wish you had not come so far as this, for you shall surely be overcome by him."

"Nay," said Sir Beaumains, "do not fear for me. Willingly I took this adventure upon me, and right willingly I carry it to its end. If I speed well, I free that most noble lady whom the Red Knight of the Reed Lands thus besieges. If I fall, I die as becomes a knight."

And she could not make him feel sorrow for himself.

Now the dwarf had gone on to the castle, and he brought to them food and drink from the lady, Dame Lyonesse. But as he went back to the lady he was found by the Red Knight, and was made to tell of the coming of Sir Beaumains to do battle with the Red Knight.

"Is he a good knight?" asked the Red Knight of the Reed Lands.

"I trow yes," said the dwarf. "He has done on this quest braver adventures than you have done in your whole life."

Then was the Red Knight very angry.

There was a great horn which hung upon a sycamore tree, and by this horn was the Red Knight called to meet those who would do battle with him. These had been many, and their bodies hung on the trees around, for it was the Red Knight's custom to hang brave knights on the trees.

Now Sir Beaumains rode up and blew the ivory horn so eagerly that the castle towers rang with the sound. He sounded it at noontide, when the strength of the Red Knight of the Reed Lands was at its greatest.

"Who is this that comes to his death, like so many others before him?" he cried, coming forth in his blood-red armour. And they buckled on his helmet, and brought him a shield and a red spear shining like fire in the sun. Then he leapt upon his horse, and rode into the open space under the castle walls, that all within and without might behold the battle.

Now the Lady Lyonesse looked out of the window, and she was very beautiful, and gentler than her sister. Then she beheld the knight Sir Beaumains, who fought the Red Knight with his spear, giving him mighty blows. She thought she had never beheld so goodly a knight.

As she watched, the knights broke their spears. And immediately they leapt from their horses, and, seizing their swords, ran at one another.

Till it was late in the day they fought, and all were surprised, for there never was a knight who had so long withstood the Red Knight of the Reed Lands.

When they had rested for some time, for both were weary, they began again. They were like fierce lions in the fight.

Now when the fight had lasted for a great time longer, Sir Beaumains struck the Red Knight so heavy a blow that all cried out who saw it.

Then was the Red Knight very angry, and suddenly smote the knight's sword from his hand, and dealt him a blow that sent him over.

Then cried the damsel of the quest: "Sir Beaumains, Sir Beaumains! my sister weeps and watches: do not fail her in this fight."

No sooner had Sir Beaumains heard the cry than he was upon his feet. He ran for his sword and seized it. With a mighty strength that came upon him, he smote the Red Knight so that he fell, and could not rise.

Then would he have slain him if a number of knights had not begged for his life. They made great excuses for the Red Knight, telling Sir Beaumains why he had done as he had done.

And Sir Beaumains, hearing their excuses, spared the knight.

Thereafter he unlaced his helmet to give himself air, for he was weary with much fighting. As he looked up at the window of the castle he saw there the Lady Lyonesse, and she was fair and full of joy.

And he thought how he should best tell them that he had but played at kitchen boy to find out who were his friends.

"For this lady," said he to himself, "shall be my wife."

CHAPTER XIII

THE PASSING OF ARTHUR

THE quarrel between King Arthur and Sir Launcelot, one of the bravest knights of the Round Table, became so bitter, that Sir Launcelot left King Arthur's Court and went to France, taking with him all his followers.

After some time King Arthur raised a large

army to go and fight Sir Launcelot. When he was leaving for France, he appointed his nephew, Sir Modred, to be chief ruler of all England in his absence.

Sir Modred, however, proved unfaithful to the trust committed to him, and in a short time gave out that he had received letters saying that King Arthur had been slain in battle with Sir Launcelot. He then called together a parliament, and made it appoint him king. So he was crowned at Canterbury.

But one day, word was brought to Sir Modred that King Arthur was coming home with his great army to punish the traitor. Sir Modred, therefore, gathered an army together, and marched to Dover. Sir Modred made great efforts to prevent King Arthur from landing in his own kingdom, but he was driven back, and he and his army were defeated.

King Arthur was much grieved, when the battle was finished, to find his beloved nephew, Sir Gawaine, lying in a boat, more than half dead. "Alas! Sir Gawaine, my sister's son," said King Arthur, "here now you lie, the man whom I loved most in the whole world. Sir Launcelot also I have lost so that now there is no joy left me on earth."

" My death is now at hand, as you well know," answered Sir Gawaine, "and it is due to my own rashness and wilfulness. I should like, before I die, to write to Sir Launcelot to ask him to return to England."

Then Sir Gawaine besought the King to send for Sir Launcelot, and to esteem him above all other knights. A little while after Sir Gawaine died, and the King gave orders for him to be buried in a chapel within Dover Castle.

Immediately afterwards, at the head of his army he marched to Barham Down, where a great battle took place. Sir Modred was again defeated, and he and his army fled to Canterbury. As the result of this victory a great number of the people joined King Arthur.

It was arranged that the next battle should take place on a level stretch of ground near Salisbury. Sir Modred raised most of his army from London and the east of England, and all those who were in favour of Sir Launcelot also joined his side.

On the night before the battle, King Arthur had a wonderful dream, in which it seemed that Sir Gawaine came to him and warned him to put off the battle on the morrow.

"If you fight to-morrow," said Sir Gawaine, "as you have arranged, you and a great number of your followers must be slain. But if you put off the battle for a month, Sir Launcelot with all his knights will come to your assistance, and you will gain a great victory over Sir Modred."

The King now called a meeting of his knights and lords, and told them of his vision, how that Sir Gawaine had warned him that if the battle was fought on the morrow he would be slain. They therefore agreed that two nobles and two bishops should go to Sir Modred and try to make a truce with him for a month.

The next day, when the armies stood face to face, Sir Modred sent word to King Arthur, asking him to meet with him in a space of ground in full view of either army, and each to bring with him fourteen knights. The King agreed to this.

Before going to meet Sir Modred, the King warned his army that if they saw any sword drawn they were to come on and slay the traitor Sir Modred, as he put no trust in him.

Sir Modred in the same way gave orders to his army. "If you see any sword drawn," he said, "come on and slay all that stand before you, for I have no faith in this truce."

After the two leaders had spoken together for some time, they came to an agreement. Then they sat down to partake of some refreshment.

When they were thus engaged, an adder came out of a bush and stung one of the knights in the foot; and he drew his sword to kill the adder, without thinking of the harm he was doing.

But when the two armies saw the sword drawn, they blew trumpets and horns, and raised a great shout. Before anything could be done, a fierce fight between the two armies began, and lasted till sunset. Great was the slaughter on both sides, and King Arthur was sorely vexed when he saw the field covered with the dead bodies of so many brave men.

Of all the King's army, only the King and two of his knights, Sir Lucan and his brother Sir Bedivere, were left. Where are all my noble knights?" he cried, as he looked around. "Alas! that I should have lived to see such a sad day; now I shall soon die, but I wish first to punish the traitor Sir Modred, for it is he who hath caused all this mischief."

Looking up, he saw Sir Modred leaning on his sword beside a great heap of the dead.

"Give me my sword," said the King to Sir Lucan, "for yonder I see the traitor"

The two knights tried to prevent him from going against Sir Modred, and reminded him of Sir Gawaine's warning.

But the King would not be persuaded. So having got hold of his sword, he ran towards Sir Modred, crying: "Traitor, now is your death-day come!"

When Sir Modred heard King Arthur, he ran towards him with his sword drawn in his hand. Then the King pierced him through the body with his sword. When he felt that he had received a deadly wound, he struck King Arthur a heavy blow on the side of the head.

Thus Sir Modred lay dead on the earth, and the King fell in a swoon at his side. The King's two faithful knights, Sir Lucan and Sir Bedivere, raised him from the ground, and quickly carried him to a little chapel not far from the sea side.

"It is best," said Sir Lucan to the King, "that we should take you to some town."

"That is true," said the King, "but I cannot stand, my head aches so much."

Then the two knights took the King in their arms to carry him; but as they lifted him he swooned again, and Sir Lucan, with the effort, fell to the ground and died on the spot.

The King, on coming to his senses, began to mourn the death of so brave a knight, and Sir Bedivere wept for the death of his brother.

"Leave this mourning," said the King, "for it is of no avail either to me or to the good knight. My time on earth is passing fast. Therefore take Excalibur, my good sword, and go with it to the water side. And when you come there, throw my sword into the water, and come again and tell me what you see there."

"My lord," said Sir Bedivere, "your command shall be obeyed, and I will bring you word again."

So the knight departed; and as he walked along he noticed how the noble sword was set with precious stones.

"If I throw this rich sword into the water," he said, "there shall come no good, but harm and loss."

So he hid it under a tree, and on coming back to the King, he said he had been at the water and had thrown the sword into it.

"What, then, did you see?" said the King.

"Sir," said he, "I saw nothing but the rippling of the waves."

"That is untrue," said King Arthur; "therefore, if you love and honour me, go again, and do as I have commanded you. Spare not, but throw the sword into the water."

Then Sir Bedivere went again and took the sword in his hand; and once more he thought it a shame to throw away that noble sword. So he hid it again, and went back and told the King that he had been at the water and obeyed his command.

"What, then, did you see?" said the King.

"Sir," said he, "I saw nothing but the rippling of the waves, and heard only the moaning of the winds."

"Ah! that is untrue," said the King; "twice have you deceived me. Who would have thought that a knight so noble would have betrayed me because of a rich sword! Go again, and throw the sword into the water. Your delay is causing me much trouble. I feel death approaching. If you do not do as I command you, I shall slay you with my own hands."

Then Sir Bedivere went back again, and

took the sword in his hand. This time he threw the sword with all his might far out into the water. There arose a hand and an arm from the water and met the sword and caught it. Three times it shook the sword, and then drew it under the surface of the water.

Sir Bedivere returned to the King and told him what he had seen.

"Ah!" said the King, "help me now from this place, for I fear that I have stayed too long."

Then Sir Bedivere took the King upon his back and carried him gently to the water side.

As they drew near the edge of the water, there came towards them a little barge with many fair ladies in it. All of them wore black hoods, and when they saw King Arthur they wept and wailed.

"Now put me into the barge," said the King to Sir Bedivere; and he did so as gently as he could. Three of the ladies, who wore crowns of gold, took the King and laid him on the deck, with his head resting on the lap of one of them.

"Ah! dear brother," said this queen, "why have you tarried so long from me? Alas! this wound on your head has taken cold."

Then they rowed gently from the land, and left Sir Bedivere standing on the shore.

"Ah! my Lord Arthur," he called out, "what shall become of me, now that you have gone from me, and leave me alone among my enemies?"

"Comfort yourself," said the King; "I cannot help you, much as I should like to, for I am going to the Vale of Avilion to heal myself of my grievous wound. If you should never hear of me more, do not forget King Arthur."

As the barge moved slowly out of sight, Sir Bedivere stood watching it. Then he ran weeping into the forest.